Who's Been Sleeping In My Bed?
Patrick AUGUSTUS
Who's Been Sleeping In My Bed?
Patrick AUGUSTUS
Who's Been Sleeping In My Bed?
Patrick AUGUSTUS
Who's Been Sleeping In My Bed?
Patrick AUGUSTUS
Who's Been Sleeping In My Bed?
Patrick AUGUSTUS
Who's Been Sleeping In My Bed?
Patrick AUGUSTUS
Who's Been Sleeping In My Bed?
Patrick AUGUSTUS
Who's Been Sleeping In My Bed?
Patrick AUGUSTUS
Who's Been Sleeping In My Bed?
Patrick AUGUSTUS

Published by The X Press
6 Hoxton Square, London N1 6NU
Tel: 020 7729 1199
Fax: 020 7729 1771
Email: vibes@xpress.co.uk

Printed by Caledonian International Book Manufacturing Ltd, Glasgow, UK.

Distributed in US by INBOOK, 1436 West Randolph Street, Chicago, Illinois 60607, USA Orders 1-800 626 4330 Fax orders 1-800 334 3892

Distributed in UK by Turnaround Distribution, Unit 3, Olympia Trading Estate, Coburg Road, London N22 6TZ
Tel: 020 8829 3000
Fax: 020 8881 5088

ISBN 1-874509-93-X

ABOUT THE AUTHOR

Born in south London of Jamaican parents, Patrick Augustus has worked for many years as a musician and record producer. As well as being the author of four novels, he has written and directed several plays, is a regular newspaper, radio and TV contributor, and a founder member of *The Baby Fathers Alliance*, a pressure group for separated fathers. Aged 34, Augustus is currently living in Brixton Heights, where he is writing his next novel.

OTHER BOOKS BY THE AUTHOR

Baby Father
Baby Father 2
Baby Father 3 - Does My Batty Look Big In This?
When a Man Loves a Woman
The Complete Baby Father

This story should be a lesson to all those cheating men who still haven't learned that while they're out playing the field, they leave their women at home with love on their minds and lust in their hearts. A dangerous combination...

THE MEN

Gussie Pottinger

Beres Dunkley

Johnny 'Dollar' Lindo

Linvall Henry

1/ DO YOU MIND IF I STROKE YOU UP?

a) 'Anvil Stroke'
Bring one hand down, letting it stroke the shaft from the top all the way to the bottom. When it hits the bottom, release it. Meanwhile, bring your other hand to the top of the shaft and repeat the stroke, creating an alternating motion.

b) 'Labial Massage'
Place a well-oiled (or lubed) hand over the spot, fingers pointing towards the rear. Pull up toward the navel, and alternate hands. Explore the inner and outer lips with your fingers. Pull gently on one and then the other. Rub the outer lips gently between your forefinger and thumb, then the inner lips.

A man and a woman. Both black. Both wanting the same thing. Each desiring the other. Neither having to get up early to go to church.

It was a sultry Saturday night, so late you could almost call it Sunday morning. The whole town was creaking in its bedsprings and resounding with the echoes of moaning and groaning. On a night like this, he shouldn't have been surprised to receive the full sensual experience. Considering the message he had left on the lonely hearts line, he should have been expecting it. In response to a similarly 'teasing' ad from a 'SBF', he had replied, *'I've got the ship, you've got the harbour, what say we tie up for the night?'*

But that was three weeks ago. He hadn't heard anything back and had forgotten all about it.

Then she called late on Saturday evening, her voice purring on his mobile phone.

She apologised for the delay. Said she had received such a tremendous response to her ad (literally thousands), that she was trawling through them one by one. It had taken twenty-one days to work her way down to him.

"Better late than never," she cooed.

They chatted away. Sex talk mostly, turning each other on with innuendo, each contemplating what it would be like to grind the other, his free hand deep in his trouser pocket juggling a stonker growing longer and stronger.

"Here I am lying on my back wasting good time by talking on the phone to someone I've never even met when I'd rather be rocking steady," she said. "Why don't you come round and put us both out of our misery."

No sooner had she given him her address than she heard the sound of his receiver hitting the floor.

Traffic? What traffic? Even with the streets full of cars, it took him only minutes to reach her eighteenth floor Kennington apartment in his Porsche.

Hairspray wafted out into the landing to greet him. The door was opened by a woman with a big smile, big wide eyes and that 'something' about her that makes men agree, "I know what you mean about her."

His gaze rested longingly on her heavy breasts, enticing him. Those breasts. They were just as she had said. You couldn't help but notice them in that low-cut blouse. If you tried not to look, they simply reached out and slapped you in the face — anything to get your full attention. They had his full attention all right, for a full minute before he noticed her watching him watching them. He had felt uneasy, but he just couldn't take his eyes off them. There was something strangely familiar about those breasts.

"Are you sure you haven't been a guest on Jerry Springer?" he asked.

She must have been used to this kind of thing. You just don't walk around the streets with that chest and not know about it. Most guys believe that women with breasts like that lose their right to complain about having their chest stared at.

Her gaze turned to his crotch, checking out his package. She grinned. From where she was standing it looked dangerous! She showed him into the living room, allowing him a good angle from which to view her backside as he followed her. Talk about booty bounce! It was just as she had said it would be. She had a sweet sugar boom-boom, that was the only way to describe it. One look at that and men would go crazy — guaranteed. No two ways about it, this was the real deal.

Anyway, one thing led to another.

Out of the cracked living room window, the Houses of Parliament formed a dramatic backdrop. He was going to be making love within sight of Big Ben! Stuff like that never failed to turn him on.

Her furniture was covered in plastic. The only art in her home was on her fingernails which were longer than her fingers. She'd been wearing a weave so long she'd forgotten the actual length of her hair and, worse, she had a bad habit of sucking her tongue as she talked. In short, she was ghettofabulous. But what she lacked in savoir-faire, she made up for in dimples and batting eyelashes.

She used the excuse of showing him around the flat to take him straight to the bedroom. To his shock and surprise, her wardrobe didn't have dresses in it, but every kind of adult sex toy imaginable. There were varying types of vibrators — rigid, hard and soft and waterproof ones. There were vibrating dongs and double dongs, dildos, male pumps, butt plugs, clitoral stimulators, clitoral and vaginal bullets, eggs and strap-ons, erection keepers and 'C' rings, non-vibrating clitoral pads, vaginal balls, massage mittens and feather teasers, handcuffs and leather penis attachments.

But all that didn't matter to him. He wanted so much to reach out to that big behind as it teased and taunted his imagination, that he didn't even mind that she didn't seem to know the difference between 'ask' and 'axe' or 'film' and 'flim'.

They flopped onto the king-size bed and talked for forty-five seconds precisely before getting naked. Butt naked. Ever seen a man undress in three seconds? That's how long it took him.

She wasted little time, either. He stared down at her womanly splendour as she pushed those chocolate breasts rolled in almond dust solidly against him, making him quiver. Then her hand dived down between his legs, followed by her head. She wasn't there long before he started moaning with pleasure.

"No rush," he cried, more to himself than to her. No way would he last at this rate, he knew.

"Would you prefer me on my back or kneeling?" she gasped.

He eased her head back and told her to lie on her back and spread her legs wide.

Wonder, she did exactly as she was told.

For a moment he sat there, looking left, looking right. He just couldn't decide, so he buried his head in the middle and began kissing her breasts like he had never fondled the like before, the tip of pink tongue on soft-hard brown nipples. Then he fumbled his way rather clumsily down below in search of that magic spot. Either he was way off the mark, or here was a woman who didn't have one.

Oh well, there was nothing to it but to do it.

It was a little tricky (he smiled to himself with self-congratulatory pride) but he managed nevertheless to ease himself in. Suddenly she stiffened, as a thought interrupted her euphoria.

"Supposing I get pregnant?" she whispered, softly and sincerely.

He didn't answer. What could he say? He was wearing two condoms, how much more protection could he possible have?

Anyway, this wasn't a time for talking.

"Relax. Just close your eyes and enjoy every minute of it," he said eventually in a soothing, reassuring voice.

What more could he say? That he had made enough mistakes and had been in this game long enough that he knew you couldn't rely on a single condom? Besides, he didn't need to tell her that, in the unlikely event that there should be an accident, she could always pop out the next day for a 'morning after' pill . . .

It felt so good he thought he was going to explode with excitement. He kissed her nipples. They were finger-licking good. He pulled himself out hard and stiff and eased in again, even harder, even stiffer. In out, in out . . .

It wasn't love, but quick sex. Just what he wanted. Just what she wanted. Excited. Inserted. Exerted. Inserted. Climaxed. Dispatched. Brief and efficient.

"Don't stop, don't stop," came a desperate cry from below. "Whatever you do, don't stop!"

So he put her on her knees and served her with grace.

And then he came again.

He grasped a gasp. He had never had a climax like this before. It was as if his stomach had erupted, sucking every last seed out of his nuts. Three hundred million soldiers, marching as to war.

And they just kept on coming . . .

All in all, it must have lasted a full ten minutes.

Ten minutes?!?!

Yeah, ten minutes. The whole neighbourhood heard his cry that night. From six streets away it sounded like an American werewolf in London. From five streets away it sounded like the howl of coyotes. To say that he was knackered afterwards is an understatement. Yet he was still as hard as a rock. He knew, however, that if he so much as even thought about it, his buba would snap in two. Just like that.

Unperturbed, she took his twitching piece in her hand and guided it back towards her crotch.

"No, Shanice," he begged her. "Not just yet . . . I can't take no more."

He must have passed out, because his mind was a blank after that. He must have keeled over with a sly grin on his chops and fallen into a long and deep slumber.

In his dreams he heard an insistent banging on the front door. It seemed to go on for hours with a man shouting 'Shanice, open up this dyam door before I bruk it down!'

The banging and shouting was so vivid, so real. The next thing Johnny remembered was being woken up by the fierce barking of rottweilers.

Rottweilers?

Yeah, rottweilers. Two vicious specimens ready to tear him apart limb from limb at the word of command from their master, an ebony-skinned man dressed in black with a long scar running down the side of his face.

"Shanice, ah wha' de raas . . .?" the man barked as he

grappled with all his strength to hold the hounds back by their dog collars.

"Oh, Cutty!" Shanice jumped up from the bed, pulling the bedclothes around her, exposing Johnny's nakedness to the world. "When did they let you out?"

"Never mind that. I said, who is this ugly geezer sleeping in my bed? Me did tell you seh, yuh nuh fe bring no man inna me yard!"

As surprised as Cutty was to see some man sexing his woman, he wasn't half as surprised as Johnny was to be present at the cuckolded husband's return. Not to mention the surprise of being confronted by two bloodthirsty killers eager to rip out his hood.

Johnny just couldn't believe it.

'This is not where I want to be right now', he told himself. He prayed to God that he was only dreaming. But he knew he wasn't. This was real.

He now recognised Cutty from the photos on top of Shanice's TV in the living room, right next to the coat hanger she used as an antenna. It was one of the first things he had seen on entering her apartment. When he asked her who the ugly guy in the photo with the 'telephone receiver' scar on his left cheek was, Shanice had said, "Cutty, my pickney daddy. He was a ruffneck from when him left Jamaica, so it never surprised me when he got done for GBH. But don't mind him, he's inside. He won't be troubling us for some time."

Cutty turned to Johnny for an explanation.

"And ah who you? Eenh?"

All Johnny could utter were the words "A friend."

"Friend? Friend?!" Cutty spat the word out as if it offended him. "What are you doing with my woman, friend? Me feel to jus' scar you up!" he screamed. "Me ah go let my dogs loose. Say hello to Satan and Lucifer, you battybwoy, you!"

Johnny saw his life flash before him, the good times and the bad. He saw his children and their mothers at his graveside, all refusing to shed any tears for the father they considered wotless. Why oh why did he not leave the premises immediately when he first saw the photo of that scarfaced psycho? Even on that underexposed polaroid, it was clear that Cutty's warped smile belonged to a man with a screw loose somewhere. Johnny thought about all the times he had been warned that his inability to control his libido would be the death of him. Now he wished he had listened to his mother. No matter how sweet, the tun-tun hadn't been made which was worth losing your life for.

* * *

It was late night when private investigator Amos Butler parked his Suzuki Vitara on the main road in Peckham. As usual, a posse of youths were standing on the corner, just loafing. Despite his undercover vehicle, they eyed the private eye suspiciously. The fact that he raised his hand in a friendly gesture towards them made them even more suspicious.

Amos felt no way, he was used to it. Some youths

had every reason to be wary of him, because one day he might come looking for them.

He killed the engine and wound down his window. A smile spread across his face as he looked up at the four-storey Victorian building opposite and saw what he had been waiting for.

It was the fourth time that day that he had returned to his stakeout. He had burned a couple of hours in the morning. Waiting. A couple of hours in the afternoon, too. Then he had passed through in the evening. Now he was back like a thief in the night. Yet still, he had seen no sign of his man.

This time was different, though. There was a faint light in the building. A shimmering silhouette. There was definitely someone in there.

The voice of Dr. Love-Jones oozed out of the car radio, deep and sensual, taking his listeners on the usual nightly ride through the steamiest tunes on the planet, with words that were guaranteed to get you panting with anticipation. Especially if you were home alone with nobody to call your own.

Amos smiled. He himself was a fan of the good doctor and tried never to miss a show if he could help it. He took a bite from the sandwich on his dashboard, then grabbed his thermos and poured out a mug of Ovaltine which he had made earlier with lots of condensed milk. Nice and sweet the way he liked it. The way he liked everything, not least his women.

As he drank, he pulled out the box file on the back seat and studied the face on the photograph again. He wondered how it was that this loser had managed to convince any woman to have children by him. Amos pitied the children. Not just because their father had done a disappearing act leaving their mother holding the can. That was the least of their worries. He pitied them because they would forever more have to live with their absent father's features on their countenance. In a sense, these children had been double-cursed.

It was the same every time. Since he started doing this job he had been amazed at how many women (not least black women, though not exclusively so) were prepared to fall for that same old 'okey-doke' from a man who pledged love for ever more. Time and time again, it was the same thing. All right, so a lot of these women were young when they got conned, too young to know about the ways of the world and how men really behaved. But that was no excuse in Amos's opinion. Women were always complaining to him about how they had been abandoned by their baby father, and he was always wondering why they found that so surprising when they had made such bad choices to start with. Take this bwoy. You could tell from looking at his shifty eyes in the photograph that he had no intention of hanging around too long once he had got his leg over. Still, if it wasn't for such guys, Amos would be out of business. Tracking down runaway baby fathers was well paid work if you could get it, especially if you worked on percentages.

Amos always worked on percentages.

He looked up at the building again. He could just

about make out a pair of legs pointed upwards, rocking back and forth gently.

He scratched his crotch absently, a wicked grin across his chops. People were always telling him that what he did for a living was dirty, depraved or perverted. At times like these he had to agree. When your job consisted of snooping around people's private lives, you often found yourself being a silent spectator to their sex lives. In his view, it was impossible watching others doing the down and nasty without wanting a spoonfull of sugar, too.

The voice of the doctor oozed through the speakers of the car radio:

Whether you're listening from your bedroom or sitting in your car, kick back, relax, and just go down low . . . This one's going out to all the phone line massive. Hold tight Gemma from Acton, hold tight Donna, Shauna and Latonya . . . Let me hear you moan and groan with pleasure . . . 'Cause the doctor is in the house. You get me?

* * *

"That's good, real good . . . Now spread your legs wide. Yeah, that's right. Nice, nice. Touch your toes. Nice and wide . . . Good. Now turn around, all I want to see is booty and elbows. Nice, nice . . ."

The twins looked really sexy together. The dreadlocked photographer splashed some water on their t-shirts. It looked very becoming. 'Yeah,' he was thinking, 'if I were on you I'd be coming, too . . .'

If truth be told, Linvall wasn't too happy about the way his career had panned out. He who had once been on his way to fame and fortune as a top fashion photographer was now reduced to this . . .

"Nice smile, now show me some tit. Yeah. Get them out for the lads. Nice. Yeah, hold it just one moment longer. Great. Nice."

He never dreamed he would have to stoop so low, but times were hard and he was grateful for the work wherever it came from. Last winter had been particularly rough. He hadn't earned a penny. From November right through to January, all he had managed to do was grow his funki dreds a few inches until now his head was adorned with a full mane of mature 'natty congo' dreads.

Taking nude pictures of models for the internet porn industry paid the rent and fed his pickney. End of story. There seemed to be a never-ending demand for fresh hardcore on the web. He had to leave his ego at home and just get on with it. Someone had to satisfy that hunger, it might as well be him. He had even convinced himself that there wasn't much difference between taking nude pictures of models for stylish fashion magazines and doing it for the net. Oh yes, there was one difference — the models in *Vogue* and *Cosmopolitan* didn't have to spread their legs wide.

Natasha Henry was a cute little model. Too short to do the catwalks, she had long since accepted the plain fact that if she was going to have any success in the industry, it would be nude. Had no qualms about it. It was business. Pure and simple. She had even gone so far as to enlarge her breasts for the purpose. The silicone was worth every penny she paid her Harley Street consultant, because the work had come flooding in since she ballooned into D-cups.

Linvall's relationship with Natasha had blossomed so much since they started working together that he had become like a best friend for her to confide in. He knew all about her two-timing boyfriend, and he knew that all she was interested in was eating without gaining weight, having a great body, smelling of roses courtesy of some killer perfume, and all the other expensive things in life. He didn't need to offer her anything, though, because he was supplying her with enough work to live it up in style. If nothing else, she owed him.

Of course Linvall fancied her, he was a man after all. What's more he knew that she was up for a little slap and tickle. They had almost succeeded in doing the nasty at the last photo session, but were rudely interrupted by Linvall's wife, who "happened to be passing" and felt compelled to drop by. Marcia must have smelled the erotic tension between photographer and model miles away. After giving her husband a hard slap, she told Natasha in no uncertain terms that she was a 'nasty bitch'. "Why don't you get your own man? Why do you want to go and mash up my marriage, you slut?"

Fortunately, Natasha was so used to the jealousy of women she considered less attractive than herself that she had forgiven Linvall his wife's outburst.

"So what do you want me to do now, Lin?" Natasha asked.

He was miles away, wondering how long it would take before he got into bed with her. He watched her mouth as she spoke and felt himself getting hard as he contemplated a blowjob. This was a girl who could really get her teeth into him. He was going to give her the length and strength. Definitely. The only problem was her twin sister, Nancy, who she had brought along for the session. What was he going to do about her?

Despite the overwhelming evidence to the contrary, not all men are cretins deserving the contempt of women. Though, the way some fellas act, you would be forgiven for thinking otherwise.

Take Linvall for instance . . .

He was of the opinion that any woman who would invest three grand to go and get her boobs enlarged had to be lacking some of those essential brain cells. But he had to admit that, now they were done, Natasha's boobs looked fine. As a matter of fact, they looked damn good.

No, not all men are cretins, but Linvall might well have to be entered into that category. Imagine, he was only moments away from pulling his first illicit snatch in ages, when he had to go and open his big mouth.

"I suppose a threesome with you and your sister is out of the question?"

Natasha was incensed.

"I can't believe you just said that," she shouted. "How dare you."

She would have stabbed him in the eye with her

fingers if he hadn't put his hand up in defence.

"I was only joking, for crissakes," he cried out. Then he paused, and with a toothy grin said, "Unless the answer is 'yes', in which case, can I videotape it?"

This time she didn't miss. She got him in both eyes — a finger in each.

"Aaaaaargh, I'm blind, I'm blind, I can't see!" he screamed. He could feel something wet and sticky oozing down his face. "I'm bleeding to death, oh my god . . ."

He was crying out to himself, though, because Natasha had already gone off in a huff, taking her sister with her. There would be no veggie for Linvall tonight, either. No, no, no. Not at all.

* * *

He made a quick mental calculation of the amount of cash he expected to get from this mission. It brought a smile to his face.

"Ain't no shame in this game," he decided.

It was not the kind of building usually associated with the hunt for an absentee father. But Amos had met all sorts in this business and, frankly, nothing surprised him anymore. He had been in the game for five years now and business had never been better. He was in a booming industry. It seemed like men just couldn't control their libidos and were always spreading their seed here there and everywhere. It seemed like the world was full of angry baby mothers wanting to get even with their baby fathers, wanting to make them pay for their misdemeanours. Now he had more work than he could handle and his reputation for hunting down runaways was increasing by the day.

Most people thought it was a crazy idea at the time. They said Amos didn't stand a chance in tracking down Claude, his sister's absentee baby father, who had done a runner and refused to come correct even when his son, Amos's nephew, was suffering from a life-threatening blood disease for which a donation of blood marrow from his father was the only hope. Believing that this was just another trap his baby mother was setting to try and catch him, Claude stayed aloof, determined to prove that his baby mother and the CSA were not going to succeed in taxing him for child support. The national newspapers soon picked up on the story and dubbed Claude the worst dad in Britain for not coming forward to save his yout'.

Amos was good at his job. He had developed a shield of muscle by spending hours in the gym body-building, and had practiced a few menacing expressions in front of the mirror. All in all, it took him three months to flush Claude out and bring him in like a bounty hunter with his prey. For Amos, a certain rush of adrenaline went with that feeling. He had learned the art of tracking down a man. He had played on Claude's greed and had set up a 'sting' by putting an ad in his favourite black newspaper to inform him that he had won some money in a prize draw, and all he had to do was come forward to collect it by the end of the week, otherwise the money would be given to charity. Sure enough, our runaway baby father had shown up at the appointed place talking about, "Where's the loot?"

Amos showed him where the loot was all right, by giving him a swift kick up the backside for his efforts. He unfortunately had to give him another kick in his seed to calm him down. It pained Amos to do it. A kick in the seed is not funny to any man, not even the man who has to administer it.

Who feels it knows it. Amos had a score to settle. Claude had dissed his sister. Besides, Amos felt he had to pay Claude back on behalf of all the positive brothas who were getting such a bad reputation for themselves all because of the worst dad in Britain.

"You're letting the whole side down," Amos told him regretfully. "Right now, what the black family needs and what black women and black children need more than anything is love."

Hunting down brothas was a job you couldn't do without taking it personally as a black man. You soon discovered that the newspapers and the rest of the media weren't kidding when they said that this problem of absentee fathers is particularly rife amongst the African-Caribbean man.

Though the ladies loved Amos and cheered him on wherever he went, there were a lot of fathers who weren't very happy about his behaviour or his community awards for services. It was even rumoured that he might be rewarded by the Queen in the next New Year's Honours List.

* * *

People assumed that Caroline and Beres were back together again, but they were just cool. Sure, they were still legally married and, sure, they were living together. Or, rather, he was living with her. But they were simply going through the motions.

Caroline had moved out of her ex-husband's house in Tooting and bought a loft in the up-and-coming Coin Street block overlooking the Thames at Blackfriars. Though reluctant at first to, once again, live under the same roof as the man who had dogged her, Beres had made her feel so sorry for his homeless self that, against her better judgment, she had agreed to rent him some space until he found somewhere else to live or her son came back from boarding school at the end of term, whichever was the soonest. In her view, space was just space. Nothing more, nothing less.

Beres, on the other hand, from the day he moved in, would have preferred to get up close and personal and see a lot less space between them. He still hoped that she was just angry at his attempted infidelity and that they would get back together again soon, back to the ways things used to be. He was not necessarily stressing her to have sex with him, but he made it clear that he wouldn't object.

Caroline refused to give him a squeeze. Why should she? She was doing all right without him and had managed to keep her head up when the chips were down.

Though he would be too ashamed to admit it, when it came to begging a squeeze, Beres was just a pussy. No doubt about it, this man could beg, but he was subtle.

He started by appealing to her ego with nice comments about how irresistible she looked. Then he succeeded in stroking and arousing her libido by exploiting the weak spot at the back of her neck.

It took forty days exactly. Beres remembered because he had been ticking off every celibate day on his calender. It was getting to him, as it does to a man after about the thirty-eighth day. Then suddenly one night, with a few glasses of champagne to loosen her up, Caroline left her bedroom door wide open as she undressed. When Beres first looked she was topless!! The next time he looked she was walking around naked. With her back to him, she bent over, almost touching her toes, apparently oblivious to his gaze.

Then she got a bikini from her drawer and proceeded to slip them on with Beres oggling her like a man who had been lost in the wilderness for years. She didn't seem embarrassed. In fact, if he wasn't mistaken, that was a look of desire in her eyes.

Then she came out in her bikini and asked Beres whether he liked what he had seen. Of course he said yes. She licked her lips and asked him if he wanted to see more. All he could do was shake his head like a dumb animal.

Taking pity on the dumb animal, Caroline took him by the hand and led him to the futon in the living area.

She poured herself another glass of champagne. Then she took him by the other hand — the hand that was hiding the erection that he had been trying to cover up.

"What are you trying to conceal?" she asked teasingly.

Embarrassed, Beres said nothing. She knew how sensitive he was to comments about his erection, so she let it drop.

They sat there, really close, side-by-side, enjoying each other's company for hours. Both with mischievous glints in their eyes. Both waiting for her to say the word.

He asked her how come women get away with everything and most men don't? "Answer me that if you will."

She replied, "All women want to possess a man and not share him. It is a primeval biological need. If this need is not satisfied, she builds a desire to avenge herself."

After drinking a few more glasses of champagne, Caroline started to purr and said, "I honestly thought that I was a strong woman . . . Okay, you're not my lover anymore. I'm glad. But sometimes I do miss the fun we used to have together. Not least the great sex."

She gave him a kiss on the forehead. Then she smiled and kissed him on the lips. They stood there kissing for several minutes — French style — like they never had before. Her tongue in his mouth brought such sweet memories.

A little apprehensively, she pulled him closer towards her.

The kisses got more and more passionate. After a while she simply stated that she felt they had been kissing long enough and that it was time to move things to a sexual intercourse level.

She got up and slowly removed her clothing in perfect silence. She pulled down her top, followed by her kinky bra, exposing her breasts and rubbing her nipples.

Pleasure is such an aphrodisiac. It was the first time he had seen her topless in months. He marvelled. She really was beautiful.

By now she was almost naked. He still had everything on. She told him to pull her panties off but, of course, he didn't need to be asked.

He must have been daydreaming for a second, because he suddenly felt her hands on him as she relieved him of his threads, garment by garment. She unbuckled his belt and undid his jeans then pulled them off his ankles along with his trainers. She could tell that he was very excited because his tone popped out just as she was about to pull down his Calvin Klein's.

Caroline stood up and led him to the shower, groping as the warm water ran. She could feel each drop splash onto her body. Slowly, she massaged away the water from around his moustache, then reached down with one hand and started tugging faster and faster, his heart beating faster and faster. It was a wonder that he was going to last at all.

Suddenly she stood up, looked in his eye and simply said:

"Eat me."

It was an order.

He held her hand, then kissed his way down to 'heaven', using his tongue for all it was worth until she finally grabbed him by the ears and pulled him up for a passionate embrace.

Beres felt sure he would explode if he was unable to release his load immediately. He lifted her up and lowered her down, guiding his tone between her thighs. It was the most incredible feeling. When she was all the way down he simply waited, holding her tightly, warm water splashing all around.

Then they started rocking. Slowly at first, in a little motion, until he found the right rhythm. He went even deeper, tickling her belly-button from the inside. His arms ached from supporting her, but he felt his orgasm starting and knew it wouldn't be long before sheer ecstacy would bring this session to a satisfactory end. He squeezed her tightly in anticipation, the wetness warm on her thighs, his seed rushing forward inside him like a raging river.

It wasn't long before Caroline came. Not once or twice, but six times in total. He was still deep inside her with a roguish smile on his face as he flicked her nipples with his tongue. She looked into his eyes and, unable to contain herself any longer, simply gasped, "Damn, that was good. I completely forgot what I was missing."

Now that she was satisfied, Beres felt no compunction about satisfying himself. He continued in a steady motion. Then he changed the tempo, increasing and slowing it at will. All the time he felt like he was about to, but he actually didn't.

He couldn't understand what was happening. Caroline had never looked so sexy. He had never felt so horny. Yet, he couldn't put the two things together to equal ejaculation. His mind drifted, unable to stay on the subject. He could have been anywhere.

Half the night later, he was still trying to solve the conundrum. They had moved from the shower to her bedroom, where the five-hour ride became even more interesting.

By now, Caroline had climaxed innumerable times and she simply lay on her back gasping for air, ready to call it a draw. If anything, Beres was even more excited than before, but he just couldn't produce the goods. Each time he failed he told himself, "It will happen next time."

Unfortunately, it didn't.

Caroline waited and waited and waited for him to hurry up and get it over with and, meanwhile, informed him of a crack she had just noticed in the ceiling.

Just as Beres was about to try once again, he felt her fingernails dig deep into his inner thigh.

Aaaaaargh!

"Don't be greedy," she told him. "Enough is enough for tonight."

When Caroline woke up the next day, her hand wandered over to the side of the bed where Beres had been sleeping, but where he had lain was now empty. She sat up, crossed her knees. Her nightie slid back, showing dimples on her thigh. She sat there for a few minutes collecting her thoughts, before wandering through the apartment looking for Beres.

Where was he? Where had he disappeared to?

Anxious to solve the mystery of his unforthcoming orgasms, Beres had gone for an early morning jog after downing some raw eggs and dipping his testicles in a bucketfull of ice. He didn't return until he had run a half marathon. Then, at his insistence, he and Caroline tried it again.

Every which way. Down on her knees, down on his knees, she touched her toes and he touched his, upside down, around and around, then they rolled over into a side by side '69'.

Beres reached into his bag of tricks for anything that would get his rocks off real quick. But whereas Caroline could climax in about thirty seconds without losing a beat, Beres could do everything but go 'all the way'.

In the ensuing weeks they did it like bunny rabbits and have been doing it ever since. In fact, they are doing it right now, even as these words are being written, but Beres just can't seem to get no satisfaction. He has made love to Caroline over two hundred times in the last few weeks and has not succeeded in ejaculating once. He considers himself too young to try Viagra, but has tried it as well. To no avail. Sadly, he's now taken to faking his orgasms (something he'd never have dreamt in a million years that he would ever do), just to save face and because he doesn't want Caroline blaming herself for his inability to produce the goods.

If only Beres had known that his enjoyment was the last thing on Caroline's mind.

Caroline was very beautiful and very smart, Beres had to give her a big shout for that. She was just his type — intelligent, attractive, and seriously successful in her legal work.

Women like that didn't cross a man's path every day. When they went out to various buppy do's together, brothas would whisper in his ear and leave him in no doubt that they were standing waiting to pick her up the moment he slipped up.

There was no need for anyone to tell Beres what a catch he had in Caroline, yet still he realised that he loved his first wife more. He felt guilty, but he who had only recently been so sex-starved that a slight wind would give him a boner, was now having to ask Caroline to put his money where her mouth was before he would feel the least bit interested. Whereas, the very thought of his first wife touched him in places that Caroline failed to reach.

* * *

Not to swell the egos of all the wotless baby fathers out there, the reason the mothers wanted Amos to hunt their baby father down wasn't because they wanted the wotless geezer back. *Au contraire.* Most of them would rather lead their lives without him. But some of them wanted their child to know its father, they considered it important, especially when it was a boy child. However, a small percentage of the women who employed him, Amos knew, only did it out of sheer vindictiveness to bring their absentee baby father to book and make him pay for his misdemeanours. Frankly, the CSA was not doing its job. Not only was it under-resourced, it seemed hardly interested in making these men suffer as these women would have them do. At most, the CSA sent someone round to the baby father's previous address only to hear that the bloke has already absconded. They would then jack in the hunt, unless the baby father was prepared to give himself up voluntarily. Now you know that's never going to happen. That's why it was best to call in an expert. Who better than Amos, having himself fathered 24 children (all girls) by 23 different women. He had previously even been on the run for many years. Not because he didn't want to be with his children, but due to unforeseen circumstances. He had gone underground — deep underground — to get himself out of the mess he had got his life into.

Yes, Amos knew the life of a baby father on the run, he knew what their every move was even before they had considered the options. He was the ultimate baby father. "I'm a professional!" he kept reminding himself. In this game, you had to be professionally trained and know how to diffuse a situation, more than just playing macho man. At the same time you had to be prepared to bash someone in the skull when necessary. So he had, even at his late age, taken up thai boxing and become a proficient martial arts man to protect himself from the seedier end of the business where baby fathers carried guns, knives and bottles. Stuff like that made his job stressful.

* * *

"Yaow, me like dat ring 'pon your finger, y'know" Cutty said, pulling out a ratchet from under his jacket.

Johnny didn't need to be asked twice. He pulled the ring off fast and handed it to Cutty.

Another day another dollar. Cutty didn't even bother to ask any further questions. He didn't want to hear any more confessions, only suggestions as to what he was to do with this raas who he caught red-handed doing the nasty with his missus.

"I get back from my little vacation, and what do I see but some man getting his banana peeled at my expense. You know how long I was looking forward to giving you the old rookoonbine, Shanice?" he was saying. "I would have preferred if you slept with my dogs than this wotless bwoy."

With Satan and Lucifer sitting dutifully at their master's feet (yet ready to obey their master's voice), Cutty sparked a blunt. Johnny tried to talk his way out of the situation.

So, was it all worth it? Was this passionate session with Shanice worth losing his life for, Johnny wondered.

Cutty was in two minds as to what to do. He really wanted to set his rottweilers on the bwoy He wanted Satan and Lucifer to tear up his balls — chew them off completely. But Johnny had just made him a cash offer he couldn't refuse.

* * *

Meanwhile, Amos was ready to pounce on his prey. He had seen the two pretty twins come storming out of the building. He had waited for several more minutes. Maybe half an hour. The light had gone off inside the building, then the front door opened again. He recognised the dreadlocks from the photo. At last, his manhunt was at an end.

He eased himself out the car and called across the road:

"Eh bwoy, yuh wanted. Yaow, Johnny Dollar, time's up! You gwine come quietly, or are you going to make me lose my temper an' bruk yuh backside? You decide."

Linvall spun round to see the detective walking towards him. He didn't know what this was all about, all he knew was that it was a case of mistaken identity.

"Johnny Dollar?" Linvall repeated. "No, sorry, mate, you've got the wrong bloke."

Amos had heard it all before. The first thing a hunted baby father always did when he was tracked down was to deny, deny and deny.

"Sure, sure, tell that to the judge," he said, then kissed his teeth. "Right now, all I'm interested in is that you put your backside in the rear of my motor. Don't make me have to get evil on you."

Linvall was nervous. This sounded serious. He didn't intend to hang around to find out what the mix-up was.

2/BARKING UP THE WRONG TREE

a) 'Climbing the Mountain'
Take the shaft in one hand and gently, sensuously, caress it for about ten seconds, then give it one quick up-and-down stroke. Repeat the sensuous caressing for about ten seconds (perhaps using slow up-and-down strokes), and then give the shaft two quick up-and-down strokes. Repeat the caressing, then give three quick strokes, etc.

b) 'A One and a Two and a Three'
Try inserting your first two fingers in, then arch your thumb back hitch-hiker style and thrust in until your thumb rests against the clitoris. You can use a variety of thrusting and twisting motions in this position. You can also vibrate your entire hand.

Most sistas thought it was a shame that Augustus Pottinger only dated white women. Mutterings of "Such a pity" and "What a waste" often accompanied the teeth-kissing posse who cut their eyes at him whenever he had the temerity and the downright insensitivity to show his caucasian persuasion at a 'man auction'.

It wasn't that sistas had anything against white women. On the contrary. It was just that Gussie was hot property in an ever-diminishing pool of single black men. The kind of man most sistas would cry for and lie for and damn-near die for.

He wasn't bad looking, but vain enough to make the

most of what he had. Six-feet two, dark like Buju, his shaven head showed off a perfectly formed skull and a chiang-kai-shek beard and moustache combination. In the old days, people mistook him for Michael Jordan, but he had heard so many women say "You look just like Tupac" so many times recently, that it swelled his head to think that he was looking younger and younger. As if to underline the similarity, he rarely wore more than a tight white vest above the waist since recently losing weight and getting into shape with regular visits to the gym.

Gussie didn't just have the looks and the physique, he also had 'potential' and was carving a niche for himself in the hustle-hustle-hustle of life. Thanks to the jewellery store he owned, he could load up with diamonds, no problem. In short, he wasn't your average black man, not in any sense of the word.

Gussie wasn't blind, he could appreciate a good-looking quality sista when he saw her. He had always had a weakness for a sista with a couple of good lines to spin and some nice clothes, good hair, and a Wrigley's spearmint fresh breath. Were it his desire, he could have had his pick of them, but he had made too many mistakes in that department in the past and had suffered so much personal hardship, he had decided to 'cross the tracks'. He was just too wary of sistas to trust himself to choose another one. If he really wanted a relationship that lasted, he decided, he had to stop dating sistas, because they were fatal for him.

Besides, his recent penchant for ladies of the 'fairer'

sex was proving too hard to resist. Right now his world was white and so was his taste.

Sistas, however, weren't prepared to let this one go that easily. It irked them that they had to compete with their white 'sisters-in-spirit', but they nevertheless challenged him when the opportunity arose. Was he suffering the delusion of self-hatred, they asked. Was he dissing his own mother? Or was he just being selfish by not doing his duty as a man in a world full of so many single black women all on their lonesome?

Gussie had tried to defend himself. But he couldn't be totally honest. How could he tell them the truth? Hoping they would appreciate a poetic turn of phrase, he offered up this explanation:

"The ways of the heart are a mystery to all."

The sistas snapped back, "What's love got to do with it?"

True, love had little to do with the fact that an endless stream of ladies were determined to challenge Gussie to 'go black and you won't go back'. As determined as these sistas were to test him, he was equally determined not to take up the challenge.

Not that he had anything against black women *per se*. On the contrary. He had been out with black women and he'd been out with white women and, as far as he was concerned, there was essentially little difference. Maybe he could reason with sistas on a cultural level in a way that he couldn't with white women but, on the other hand, white women were generally happy to take you as you were (warts and all) whereas a sista was determined to get all in your mind and mess up your vibes.

His experiences over the last couple of years with sistas had been enough, more than he could take. He had been wounded in all the places that really hurt a man — in his heart, in his soul, and below the belt. He had lost his faith in black women, abandoned his hope of spending the rest of his life with one. As far as marriage was concerned, he had made up his mind that there would be no black in his union, Jack.

However bad and mad the sistas got with Gussie, it was nothing compared to how vexed and cantankerous many brothas felt at the very thought of Carmel De Souza giving it up to a white guy. They just couldn't handle the fact that this veritable jewel of the Nile had turned her back on 'the world's greatest lovers' for some jungle fever. It was cramping their style. Some of 'the Caribbean's finest' had murderous intention in their eyes if ever the subject came up for discussion. Quite simply, it burned brothas to see a white guy with a crisser gal than they themselves had. They couldn't come to terms with it. It was an affront to their manhood, they claimed, at the same time absolving themselves of all responsibility for their actions should they actually buck up on Carmel walking hand in hand with some white guy on the street.

It wasn't that they had anything against white guys, they insisted. For, though it took them a long time to come round, most black men (with the exception of a hardcore south-east London crew) had by now accepted the fact that some sistas simply preferred white guys and there was nothing they could do about it. What burned a lot of brothas was that Carmel was the daughter of the late J. Arthur De Souza.

Many were those men who hoped that they would be the one to teach her how to make love to a black man without ever being tired. Try as hard as they could, however, there had been no official record of Carmel ever dating a man who was made in the shade.

As luck would have it, the opportunity of being the first of his race to get a look-in fell on Gussie. His eyes had widened with interest when she was introduced to him at a dinner party hosted by one of his new Notting Hill set. Everything about her seemed so white that Gussie became virtually colour blind. As far as he was concerned, Carmel was black only on the outside. Apart from that, she so perfectly walked the walk and talked the talk that many of his white friends did, that he believed she was indistinguishable from them.

A few days later, he had bumped into her at an eaterie in Covent Garden favoured by the arty crowd. He knew straight away that it would take more than his usual 'Your place or mine?' play to succeed with her. She looked like the type of who has heard every line in the book. Women like Carmel didn't fall for that old okey-doke any more. He had to take his time, hold his breath, wait to exhale and exaggerate about how well his business was doing, and how much money he was making.

As luck would have it, she said that he had an

interesting face, and would he model for her. Only it wasn't his face she was interested in.

Even dressed in her oversized paint-spattered blue overalls, which did their best to disguise her femininity, it was clear that Carmel had class and pedigree, both of which Gussie found irresistible. There was something about the way she held her head high (a little too proudly), confidence oozing like she knew she was a priceless jewel in the crown.

"Keep still," she rebuked. "I won't be much longer."

But it was too late. Standing before her like a frozen statue, Gussie could feel his manhood letting him down as it rose upwards before him, as if defying gravity. They say that black folk don't blush. Well, it's not true. Gussie didn't know which way to turn, couldn't move even if he knew. It wasn't so much a stonker as a gobstopper. Huge. It felt heavier than it had ever felt before. He tried to think of England, of soccer and of Iron Mike, but none of that had a diminishing effect on his bedroom bully. At least, he didn't think it did.

Carmel didn't seem the least bit fazed by it, but sketched away as if she had seen it all before, her eyes flitting continuously between model and canvas.

"Relax," she encouraged. "Just another five minutes."

Those five minutes seemed like five hours. Why, oh why would his stiffie not disappear?

Gussie had no problem with stripping naked in the name of art. During his college days, posing nude for local evening classes was a lucrative way of supplementing his meagre grant. Back then, his shlong had behaved itself, refusing to stand to attention in a room full of strangers. He had seen it as a job, pure and simple, and had been paid for his efforts. This time, though, he was doing it for free, as a favour to the woman he already knew he wanted to marry.

He knew she wouldn't cook for him. Women of Carmel's social class simply didn't cook for their men any more. Carrying devotion that far had gone out of fashion. Besides, Carmel had more important things to do with her time. She was a new type of woman who intended to live her life to the max fulfilling her ambitions, not slaving over a hot stove for any man.

Still he wanted her.

She was the kind of woman he needed in his life, a classy woman who could open doors for him. Highly intelligent, having seemingly read everything and been everywhere. When she started questioning you, it wasn't easy. She asked Gussie tough questions that put him on the spot, questions for which you would have to be on *University Challenge* to answer. Questions like, "So, what are you thinking?"

He hadn't wanted to say. How could he tell her that his mind was on her backside?

"What are you thinking?" she asked again, determined to know.

He laughed and said he was wondering why she was slumming it in east London when she was clearly a west London girl.

Her apartment in Shoreditch, on the fringe of the

City, was in an area with the largest density of artists anywhere in the world. All the other tenants in her building were also artisans of some sort or other — painters, sculptors, potters, fashion designers. In the penthouse suite at the top, there was even a recording studio. Moreover, it was not far from where Gussie now lived in the Docklands.

"You can see my apartment from here," he said, pointing out the window into the distance.

"Yeah, it's a great view," she nodded.

"So how long you been living here?"

It was just small talk, but he needed time. He needed to get his mind off his shlong, think about something else, distract his misbehaving pecker for a while.

She'd been there a couple of years. The rent was cheap and with the huge windows filling the apartment with light, the place was ideal.

He noticed the lottery tickets on her table.

"Any luck?" he asked her.

She laughed and admitted that she had bought them for a laugh.

With just a couple more strokes of her charcoal, she was through with the sketch. She passed the pad over to Gussie as he quickly started putting his clothes back on.

"What do you think?"

It was an impressive likeness. Embarrassingly, she had also captured his stiffie. All he was concerned about was that she had under-represented his manhood.

"Is this some kind of modern art or something? Because you've got my dimensions all wrong," he protested.

No, she insisted, she hadn't. Everything was exactly how it was supposed to be.

* * *

Linvall now regretted having borrowed the keys to The Book Shack from Johnny. It seemed like a perfect idea at the time. Since business had been going rough, he had tightened his belt and done everything to reduce his outgoings. Including giving up his studio in Clapham. He also regretted having grown his locks back again. When his old man had reached for the dreaded scissors and trimmed him, he should have stayed trimmed. Then people wouldn't keep mistaking him for Johnny Dollar.

Once he made his fortune, Johnny lost all interest in the shop he used to run. There didn't seem much point. Brothas just didn't read. Johnny remembered hearing about how a Ku Klux Klan bloke said, 'If you want to hide anything from a black man, put it in a book.' In his years of running The Book Shack Johnny had found, to his dismay, that the KKK guy was more or less right. With the exception of a hardcore of some 5% intelligent black men (who, coincidentally, were mostly in jail), black men were usually more concerned with knowing when the book was going to come out as a 'flim'.

Linvall jumped at the opportunity when Johnny told him he could use the shop as a studio. That was before he realised that Johnny was a wanted man.

Linvall's initial meeting with Amos had not been altogether friendly. Linvall couldn't believe that a big man like Amos could run so fast. He hadn't got far down the road, when the detective wrestled him to the ground with a flying tackle that would have done any scrum half proud.

"Is why you have to mek me do that, man?" Amos asked, as if it pained him more than it pained Linvall. "Now, like I was saying, you're wanted . . ."

Amos pulled a photo of a sweet little boy of nine or ten years old out of his coat pocket and shoved it in Linvall's face.

"You've got the wrong man," Linvall blurted again. "What's wrong with you, man? I'm innocent."

He could hardly breathe. Amos had all his body weight on his victim's chest.

The realisation suddenly dawned on Amos that he really might have the wrong man.

"You're not Johnny Dollar?"

"That's what I've been trying to tell you. Jeez!"

"But you know him, right?" Amos asked tentatively, easing himself off his captive.

"Yes, yes, I know him. Just release me, let me go!"

Amos helped Linvall up off the pavement.

"So, you know where I can find him?"

"What do you want with Johnny?" Linvall asked, a hostile look on his face.

"I've got a message for him," Amos replied.

"Well give it here . . ." Linvall stretched out his hand.

"No, I can't. It's very important that I give it to him

personally."

Linvall stared at Amos and kissed his teeth as if to say, 'you must think I'm a dyam fool'. He wished that he could clout the guy, but Amos didn't look like the type of man you could give a slap to and get away with it.

"Well Johnny's not around, so either you give me the message or you can forget it."

Amos realised that he wasn't going to get much change out of Linvall. He pulled out a business card from his pocket.

"Please make sure he gets this, and gives me a call. It is a matter of utmost importance."

Linvall looked down at the card and smiled to himself.

Butler & Associates, Detective Agency, Coldharbour Lane Brixton

Available for all types of investigative work, both for the corporate and the private clientele. With our training and knowledge you can be assured of a complete value for money

service with total confidentiality and anonymity. We specialise in tracking down baby fathers.

"Look, I owe you. Maybe I could buy you a meal," Amos suggested.

"No thanks," Linvall snapped. "Yes, I should think you do owe me — an apology for a start."

"Oh did I not . . .? I'm sorry . . . I mean, I'm sorry. You know what I mean. Anyway, I'm sorry. Just sorry. Sorry."

"All right!" Linvall had heard enough. "All you owe

me now is damages in a court of law. Thanks for the business card, you'll be hearing from my solicitors."

* * *

Gussie, meanwhile, was back at his riverside apartment. Making a few calls to get the S.P. on Carmen.

"Gussie? Augustus Pottinger?"

"Who else? You sound surprised to hear from me?"

"I am."

"Why?"

"Because you never call. I'm the one who's always calling you."

"Yeah, well, you know, maybe it's time that I returned all the compliments."

Yemi was suspicious. She had by now given up totally on Gussie. She had once hoped in vain that there could be something between them. Even though Gussie had seemed just as interested in her as she had been in him, after six weeks of mad intensive love, his interest seemed to wane and he started talking about being "just good friends". She didn't let it go immediately, but pursued him a good while, with little gifts, tickets to concerts, popping round to his place unannounced with a big meal she had cooked for him, and all that sort of thing. The more she did for him, the more he took her for granted, until at the end he came right out and said, "I just don't love you any more I just don't feel the same way."

She had asked for it, she shouldn't have been

pressing him to tell her exactly what he thought. But she had done, and he had done and it had ended any feelings she had left for him. He would never know how much he had hurt her. How easily her love had turned to hate. To Gussie, toying around with her emotions was harmless, no big deal, nobody was going to get hurt. To Yemi, you couldn't just chop and change your feelings where another person's feelings are involved.

She stopped calling him after that.

"So, what exactly do you want?" she asked him.

"Just calling to see how you are doing, that's all."

"Oh, it suddenly crossed your mind after all this time to find out how I am doing?" she said, disbelievingly.

"Yes."

"Please Gussie, don't insult my intelligence."

"Yemi, correct me if I'm wrong, but I'm getting some bad vibes off you. Wassup?"

"What's up? Gussie, as I remember it, the last we spoke you made it clear to me that you didn't want to have anything to do with me."

"I didn't actually say that."

"You didn't have to."

"I still value you as a friend, I just didn't want to marry you, that's all."

"I didn't want to marry you, either. In fact, I'm just about to get married, and when I told my fiancé that I once had a t'ing with you, he made me go to the clinic for a blood test. You see, Gussie, your reputation goes before you."

"I see, so who's your boyfriend?"

"Christopher Craig, I believe you know him."

"What Chris Craig, the comedian? You're kidding me."

"Not at all. You two were at school together, weren't you?"

"Let me get this straight, Yemi, *you* are going to marry a white guy."

"Please, Gussie, this is the New Millennium, we're passed the stage where it should matter what colour our partners are."

"Yes, but it was you who was always going on about how you would never marry a white guy and how black folks got to stick together to save the black family, the black race etcetera. Remember that New Year's Eve party at Kojo's place, when I brought that white woman I was checking at the time, and you turned around and started telling me about how disgusted you were that I was dating 'the enemy'?"

"That was ages ago. Times move on, people move on and, yes, I have changed my views. Next to all the black guys one meets nowadays, white guys don't seem all that bad after all."

Gussie could not get over it. Chris Craig, who at school used to be NF.

"Look, you don't have to rush into this marriage, you know. Why don't I come by tonight, pick you up, go out for a meal. We could talk things over and, if you like, I can stop by your place afterwards. I don't mind."

She kissed her teeth loudly into the phone. "You must really think your poo don't stink. I'll send Chris your regards."

With that she slammed down the phone.

Gussie was still reeling from the revelation. For several minutes it irked him bad to think of Chris and Yemi as an item, let alone married. He could think of nothing else, until he remembered that he hadn't even garnered the information he needed from Yemi. He dialled her number again.

"I forgot to say 'congratulations'."

"Gussie, you're a pain, you know that?"

"All right, all right. But hear me out, I need something from you."

"Surprise, surprise."

"You know some artist woman called, Carmel De Souza?"

"De Souza?"

"Yeah, that's right, she went to Ellen James's at the same time as you."

"Yes, I know Carmel. Why?"

"I need to know the lowdown."

"What?"

"You know, the juice, the SP. Wassup with her?"

"Gussie, let me get this straight, you're calling me to help you with your chances of getting Carmel into bed?"

"No, not exactly . . ."

"You have got some nerve. Call me again, and I'll set the law on you."

She slammed the phone down once more.

* * *

"Beres!"

It was Grace, struggling to push a shopping cart laden with produce whilst heavily pregnant.

"Yeah Grace, what you saying?" Beres said, giving her a brief hug. "When is it due?"

Grace beamed a huge smile of pride and looked down at her heavy stomach.

"Any day now . . . and it's triplets!"

"Triplets! Boy you and that man of yours must be working overtime."

Beres, being a gentleman from time, immediately took control of the shopping trolley.

"Yes, I have a man who works overtime. That's better than some men I can mention," she said with a knowing wink.

By the look of anguish on his face, this seemed to upset Beres, and he was silent for a moment as he gathered as much air as he could into his lungs.

"I got a call last week from Sonia in Venice. She asked me to water her plants while she's away."

"Is that all she said?" Beres asked.

"Well, you know how we women are," Grace teased, "we tell each other everything. But I'm sworn to secrecy."

"Yeah, I bet."

"So, are you happy now me and Sonia are not an item any more? Isn't that what you always wanted? Now you can take care of all your runnings without any interference from me. You must be happy about how that turned out."

Beres grimaced. Grace already knew too much about his business.

"She left me, how am I going to feel good about that?" he said finally.

"Yeah, but you're a man," Grace teased, "you can get over it."

"Seriously Grace, did she say anything else to you?"

"Like what?"

"About us. Does she want to get back together again, or does she still want to swing?"

Grace looked Beres up and down as he helped her load her Fiat Punto full with shopping.

"Me sorry fe you, y'know Beres. Men like you never really understand where your women are coming from, do you?"

Beres listened. She was right of course. Beres should have accepted by now that the relationship was over. But there had to be a way.

"So, you don't think . . ." he began.

"No chance," Grace concluded firmly.

"So, you don't think you could speak to her?"

"I'll be seeing her when she gets back."

"Well, say 'hi'."

"I'll do better than that, I'll tell her that you looked miserable and sick and that you've lost a lot of weight. You do want her back don't you?"

She winked at Beres. He caught the drift and smiled.

"Anything you can do, Grace."

"Yes, well, you're lucky you have a good friend in me," she teased. "You men, one day you'll learn that your woman is your most valuable asset and then you'll take care of her."

Beres smiled, now more confident about things. If anyone could change Sonia's mind it was Grace.

"Let me tell you something about Sonia . . ." the heavily-pregnant Grace continued as she and Beres sat down to capuccinos at one of the cafés in the shopping mall. "She needs more loving than you gave her. You were crazy not devoting all your time to her when she was around. No disrespect, Beres, but you were stupid. A nice, intelligent, attractive girl like Sonia was the best woman you were going to find. Now you've lost her, it's no use crying over it."

"Just tell me straight, Grace, have I got any chance of getting Sonia back? I need her back."

Grace smiled. Beres was dependent on her now, because Sonia refused to speak to him, refused to answer her door to him, refused to take his calls. Beres needed her to relay his ex-wife's feelings. It was ironic.

"It seems like you loved her very much, yet you didn't show that in the ways she needed to see it. You can't blame me for having taken your place in her affections."

Beres winced with pain as he bit into his croissant, nearly biting off his tongue. It was going to take him a long time to forget Grace's role in his marriage breakdown. She didn't have to milk his dilemma for all it was worth.

Grace was the last person that Beres expected to be pouring out his troubles to. You see, Grace and Beres had history. Or rather, Grace and Sonia had history. Grace was the 'other' woman in their love triangle, and Sonia was her girlfriend. But now Sonia and Grace had split up. They remained best of friends, but Grace had been on a 'shopping trip' to New York and found the man that she never thought she'd find and they were going to get married before the babies were due.

So now, Beres was pursuing his ex-wife again. He had a 'jones' in his bones, that made him ache for her. The u-turn in Grace's sexual orientation gave Beres hope that Sonia would see the light and turn around, too. He was still in love with his ex. Always had been. Probably always would be. He couldn't explain why he didn't want to lose her, but right now he didn't mind taking all the distress she was prepared to dish out, if it only meant that they could all be a family again, if not for his sake, then for their daughter.

But how was he going to convince her to come back this side?

"Tell me something," Beres began, an edge of cynicism in his voice. "What do you have that I don't have?"

"I beg your pardon, I would have thought that was obvious by now."

"Yes, but you know what I mean. Apart from the physical differences, how did you treat Sonia better than I used to do?"

Grace smiled. Where should she begin?

"Well, for example, I call her regularly to see how she's doing. Now you never used to do that, did you? How could you have thrown away her love so easily, Beres? Sonia would have done anything for you. Even a blind man can see that she is worth as much love as you've got to give her."

Beres didn't need Grace to tell him that. Neither did Sonia need to leave him for another woman for him to appreciate that.

"What else?" he said flatly.

"She used to say that she felt closer to me because I always 'touched' her in a way that you never did," Grace continued.

"Oh, come off it," Beres protested. "She can't say I didn't touch her, how can you make love without touching? How can you kiss without touching? How can you sleep in the same bed without touching? That is just not true."

"Sonia doesn't mean touching her with your hand, but a much more intimate 'touch', touching her soul, her spirit. You can touch your partner with just your eyes, you know. You've heard of the 'look of love' haven't you? Now don't you think it would touch your woman in her soul if you gave her that look every morning? And you can touch her with words. It doesn't have to be any fancy words, just 'I love you' every now and then. Sonia never tires of hearing 'I love you'. And she never had to ask me to hug her, or kiss her or love her, or go out with her. I used to do all those things without being asked. Beres, your mind was so fully engrossed in your mission to be rich and successful, that you had all but neglected your woman. It was she who was always having to pressure you into going out or doing something together. You never seemed to be able to find the time."

Beres shifted uneasily in his seat. As painful as it was to hear, he wondered what exact words Grace had used to pull Sonia, and whether the same chat-up line would work for him. Why had he always held back when all Sonia needed was a gentle touch?

"You're too stiff, Beres. You're far too English for your own good. Now at least you'll know what life is really about after this," Grace said philosophically. "Put it down to experience, that's the name everyone gives to their mistakes. Your mistake was that you didn't get in touch with your feminine side. That just can't work. You can't be a slave to your masculine side and expect to fulfil the needs of your woman at the same time, that's impossible. It was great that you had ambition, and were doing what was necessary to get where you wanted to be in life. Sonia would support you to the maximum, but she didn't want you to achieve your ambition only to change along the way. That seemed to have been what was happening. Put it this way, you can live to become bankrupt several times over and bounce back each time by making fortunes several times over, your house can burn down and you can replace it, but you're never going to be able to replace a woman like Sonia."

Beres had to grit his teeth. If he wasn't such a

gentleman, he might not have been able to control his emotions quite so diplomatically. Apart from everything else, Grace didn't need to rub it in his face. Ever since he was young Beres had dreamed of becoming wealthy and finding a woman just like Sonia to share that wealth with. He had tried and failed, but he was ready to take on the world again if it would bring Sonia back where she belonged. But where was he going to find this feminine side that Grace was going on about? He was sure he didn't have a clue what she meant.

"Search for your feminine side, Beres. You'll find it in your mind, in your soul, in your dreams, in your ambitions and in your love. That's all Sonia wanted from you. She didn't care if you never had a penny, as long as you could give her your love. *Really* give her your love."

Grace looked at her watch and realised she had to leave.

"I'll call when I hear any more from Sonia," she said.

"Is there really any point in my trying to get her back or is it too late?"

"It's never too late, y'know, Beres."

Beres left money to cover the bill, and got up also.

* * *

"Nothing beats being young rich and single," Johnny smiled to himself as he pulled out the roll of notes held together with a rubber band and flicked through it with a pleasing smile. There was almost five grand there. It was his cut from the illegal weekend rave he had organised. It had been a massive success, pure roadblock. Sensational. Everybody had had a good time and all his crew got paid, so everybody was happy. He felt no way that the lion's share of the profits had gone to him either, after all the 'banker' always gets paid most. Five grand would make up for the money he had paid Cutty for his balls. Sweet.

Johnny held the wad under his nose and sniffed. 'Aaaagh!' Nothing smelt good like cash. Cash was king and in the world of money, five grand in twenties and fifties was well-respected royalty. He kissed the wad briefly before tucking it back into the black leather money belt he always wore.

To look at him, you wouldn't think Johnny was on the run. But with the Child Support Agency on his tail, Johnny realised that the only way he was going to get to keep his millions was to withdraw the whole lot in cash and to go underground. But with that much cash in a safe deposit box, you can't just 'disappear'. Johnny had set himself up as an informal black bank to help youths who were referred to him with a good business idea. It wasn't a charity or anything, Johnny took a good whack for his investments. Basically, the High Street banks simply refused to lend money to black entrepreneurs. Even when successful black businesses went to the bank with perfect business plans, all the black manager could see was a black man and, in his narrow mind, the two words 'black' and 'business' just didn't go together.

'Asian' and 'business', yes. 'Anybody else' and 'business', yes. Talk about institutionalised racism!

Johnny glanced down at his diamond-studded Cartier. It was almost midday. He looked cool in the latest model Ray-Bans. Apparently these wraparound darkers were the popular choice amongst all the rich boys over Stateside. He already had a nice car and 'nuff niceness fashionwise. He was on a successful roll and those sunglasses made him feel invincible.

He tucked the money back in his belt and tooted his horn loudly a couple of times, just for the hell of it. A delicate touch of his foot on the accelerator and the Porsche moved forward at a cruising speed.

He felt his money belt for the wad of banknotes again and pulled it out for another quick look. Pure, raw cash. He smiled a proud smile to himself.

He enjoyed modelling in his brand new sports car. It was flash and powerful, just like him. A status symbol to every black youngster that they, too, could make it.

Poverty wasn't a virtue in Johnny's view, but a vice that could lead to apathy. He couldn't stand seeing beggars because, from experience, he had learned that there was no such thing as 'something for nothing'. All you needed in life was a plan, a road map and the courage to press on to your destination with persistence and determination. "Start where you are with what you have, knowing that what you have is plenty enough," his father had always told him. Though there were no short cuts, anything the mind could conceive and believe, it could achieve. All you needed was the right mental attitude.

Johnny had the right mental attitude all right. Especially when it came to pulling women. He loved the idea of being able to bed a different woman every day. It was that sense of adventure, that sense of excitement as you're going towards the unknown. And he knew that, should an angry husband show up in the middle of things, he could afford to buy his way out of a beating by making them a financial offer they could not refuse.

Yes, there was nothing better than being young, rich and single. However, in his hurry to get out of Shanice's bed with his life in tact, Johnny made the near-fatal mistake of pulling up his zip too fast. The pain shot up from the tip of his penis through his balls, up his backside, making his eyeballs nearly pop out of their sockets. He was still sore from the experience, but not too sore to jump in bed with another woman should the occasion arise.

He was sitting at a red light with the Porsche's top down and its earth-shaking bass thumping, enjoying the attention of a group of brothas standing on the corner. Some of them pumped up their fists in respect, while others, afraid of looking impressed, assumed the gangsta stance, fiddled with their mobile phones and tried hard to appear disinterested. Johnny knew better, though. Jealous dem jealous.

Suddenly, a fly looking woman in exactly the same car with pulled up at the lights and beeped her horn.

Johnny turned around. She was looking at him like she wanted to take him, make him and break him. Her eyes were beautiful. Her face beamed in a huge smile. She looked good enough to eat, fashionably eclectically dressed for 'happy hour' with her Ray Bans resting on top of her headfull of curls. Just as the lights changed, she pulled down her itsy bitsy blouse and showed off too much of her chocolate drop flesh in a flash. Johnny liked what he saw and wanted to touch her and give her the wickedest slam there and then. And if he wasn't mistaken, she mouthed the words 'Nice car. You want a grind?'

'Naaaaah', he was thinking. He must be dreaming. Before he had a chance to respond with that engaging smile of his, she was on her way with a screech of tyres.

Johnny raced after her, punching the engine until it roared, hummed and vibrated between his legs, carrying him through the sun-drenched streets of west London. But a woman with 300 brake horse power at the tip of her toes and complete confidence in her driving abilities, was a hard act to follow. He was going to have to play catch to even get close.

* * *

He knew she was pretending to sleep. He could hear it in her breathing. Her normal breathing pattern was long, deep, slow and had a low hum, but now she was breathing in short, sharp gulps. Yes, she was definitely pretending to be asleep. Or was he just paranoid?

To be honest, Linvall was horny like hell, but he wasn't going to wake Marcia up if she really was asleep.

Patrick Augustus

He knew he would get grief. It was the third night in a row that he had come home after midnight, and he was running out of excuses. If she was asleep, then fine, he would slip into bed beside her and she would be none the wiser. What she didn't know wouldn't hurt her (or him). But if she was awake and pretending to be asleep, he was for it. That much was for sure.

He eased himself gently between the sheets, hardly breathing. She stirred. He stiffened, half in bed and half out, and watched her in the semi-darkness. Her nose seemed to be twitching in her sleep. Then she was still again, snoring gently. He waited until he was sure that she was dead to the the world before he eased the rest of his body into the bed. He had only just managed to rest his head on the pillow for a second when suddenly, Marcia sniffed twice and said, "I smell S-E-X."

Linvall held his breath. Maybe she was talking in her sleep. That was, of course, wishful thinking. He felt a dig in the ribs from the rolling pin she sometimes carried to bed with her. No, Marcia wasn't easy.

"I said, I smell S-E-X on you," she repeated, turning round and facing him with that permanent scowl on her face which she always had when it came to any questions of trust and faith.

"S-E-X? On me? No, you must be mistaken," Linvall insisted. "I ain't had none since . . . Well, you know how long it is since I had some."

"You're lying."

"No, I swear to God."

"Then what are you doing sneaking into bed at this

hour?," she kicked in. "You've been having sex with some other woman, haven't you? Come on, out with it. I smell veggie all over you. Do you think I'm stupid?"

"Awww come on, Marce. I can't see why you still don't trust me. I haven't been unfaithful for ages."

"You mean I haven't caught you for ages," she corrected. "Right, drop your pants," she ordered. "All I'm interested in is whether you've been doing any late night soldering behind my back."

Linvall couldn't believe that Marcia was going to insist on a tun-tun inspection at this time of night.

Some men believe that they are 'under manners', but as far as Linvall was concerned, no man could understand what being 'under manners' meant like he understood it. He who feels it knows it. This wasn't just your normal stress factor 'under manners'. Marcia was much more subtle than that. He couldn't even go to the bathroom without Marcia pulling out her stop watch to check exactly how long he'd been in there.

Marcia Henry considered herself the champion of all the world's wronged women. She was on a mission, not just to make Linvall pay for being unfaithful in the past, but for being a poor role model for their thirteen-year-old son Lacquan. As she was always fond of reminding Linvall, "All men are dogs and once a dog always a dog!" To the women of the world, Marcia's advise was simple: "Give a man a reason to be unfaithful, and he'll take it. The best way to make sure that your man doesn't do the doggystyle, is to never give him the opportunity. Because men can't control themselves. You have to stop thinking of your man as 'my man' and start thinking about him as 'a man', because that's how he's going to behave, not as your man. So even though Linvall's my husband and the father of my son, I watch him every minute of the day. And it works. He's tried many times but he hasn't succeeded in being unfaithful for ages."

Linvall dropped his pants reluctantly, suggesting that they take a late night shower together after. Marcia suggested that he leave the house immediately and that he take his whiff of 'P-U-M-P-UM' with him. She went for the rolling pin to emphasise the point. He saw what was coming at him and dived out of the way, looking for cover, but Marcia was too fast for him. She threw the rolling pin like a boomerang and, just when he thought he had outfoxed her, it came from the opposite direction and struck him hard in the middle of the forehead.

"Aaaaaaaaaaaaaaaaaaaaaarrrrrrrrgggggghh!"

Any man who has had to suffer physical or psychological abuse at the hands of his woman would share in Linvall's pain.

"I know what you've been up to all night, Linvall. I KNOW. And I know whose company you've been in. How is it that I know such things? Because, you see, I was there. Yes, I was there. I saw everything. My dreams don't lie. You can't deny it. Look at me in the eyes and tell me that you weren't banging away with some girl young enough to be your daughter. Come on, look into my eyes, let me see your mind, because my third eye will catch you out if you're lying."

"Fine," he said, "have it your own way.

But "Fine." was not an acceptable way to end an argument, not with a woman with a spare rolling pin in her hand. She slammed it down hard across his knuckles. He screamed with pain again.

"What do you go and do that for?"

"I said I want answers," she reminded him. "I haven't got all day. Come on, out with it."

Years of coming up with excuses always came in handy. On his way home, Linvall explained, he had fallen asleep on the night bus, and he didn't wake up until the bus had got all the way to Croydon. When he woke up, he realised that his pants felt all sticky, which was when he realised that he must have been having a wet dream, which accounts for the smell of S-E-X.

She didn't believe a word of it.

He reminded her of his suggestion that they put it all behind them and have some bathroom S-E-X. She spurned his advances. It had been a long hard day and she needed some rest. "No, not that kind of rest." She had to get up early in the morning, "I've got things to do, even if you haven't." Besides, she didn't want to mash up her new hairdo.

She was deep in thought, far away, in another realm.

The more she thought, the more he felt nervous. She was no doubt planning something, plotting something.

He couldn't hold it in any longer, he had to find out.

"What are you thinking?" he blurted, the palms of his hands sweaty and itchy .

"If I wanted you to know, I'd be talking instead of thinking," she snapped.

3/IF LOVE SO GOOD HOW COME IT HURT SO BAD?

a)'The Pressure Cock'
With one hand, pull the shaft's skin toward the base. Using the other hand, rhythmically pick various points along the shaft and squeeze gently.

b)'Close but no Cigar'
If your partner has a particular spot that they like to have caressed, try doing so very close to but not quite on that spot (except perhaps occasionally). This trick will make them take longer to reach their climax, but they will likely have a much stronger, more powerful orgasm when it finally does happen. As a variant, you can do the 'not quite on target' until they get close to coming, then switch to the target itself, thus earning their eternal gratitude.

Sometimes Johnny had to pinch himself to realise how far he had come in such a short time. Eighteen months ago he was out there on the frontline trying to make it like every other black man, and finding it a hard struggle in the ghetto. Eighteen months ago his destiny on this sceptred isle looked bleak and limited. Despite being the second generation of his family in this race-obsessed country, he was at best 'just another nigger'. But with his millions, he could be anybody he wanted to be. He had three different passports, three different identities and, whenever he flashed his cash, he got treated with respect.

It's a question of class. Johnny had turned his back on the ghetto, and he didn't intend to go back. There was no goal too great nor dream too high for him, as long as his mind could conceive and believe, he could achieve it.

"Africans built the pyramids and all the scientists, mathematicians and the geometricians say that that was impossible. So they call the pyramids one of the seven wonders of the world," his father used to tell him.

Nothing was impossible, Johnny agreed. Accordingly, he would devote a few minutes when he woke up each morning to some creative thinking — potential business ideas.

"It's all about money," his father had said. "A healthy cash reserve is the best protection against financial ruin. Money don't just increase your net worth, but helps you help others — your family, friends and everybody. You'll hear people say that money won't bring happiness, but it's brought more happiness than poverty."

His father had also said, "If you spend all day thinking about your dickie, all you are at the end of it is one big dickie." Johnny had long forgotten that part, though.

He turned right off the Harrow Road, down the Grove, the sweet sound of soul oozing from the car stereo, his mind focusing on the tightly-clad bottoms of several young ladies in mini-skirts, batty riders and leggings. He saw London as a boomtown ripe for someone like him with a head full of ideas to reap a fabulous harvest. Even though life for his father had not been a crystal stair, Johnny would still aim for the stars. He had been through failure and frustration, times when money didn't come too easily, if at all, times when the creative juices weren't flowing and times when he felt totally out of touch with the rest of humanity. But it had never once crossed his mind to jack it all in. He knew where he wanted to go and what he had to do to get there. He had that vivid picture in his mind of his goals and would simply go about the task of achieving them one by one, determined to be the best in whatever he chose to do.

As he cruised steadily down the Grove, his concentration was shattered by the ear-splitting sound of a car coming from the opposite direction, with its boom box cranked up as it played some mad underground tapes. He made eye contact with the driver. She was staring at him. He thought he recognised those dreamy eyes from somewhere. It took him a moment to register. The car! It was the woman from earlier. In the extra moment it took him to catch his breath, he was able to read her lips:

'Tickle your ass with a feather?'

He was sure that was what she said. One of the nicest things anybody had every said to him.

She tooted her horn loudly as she passed him on the other side of the road and zoomed away at law-breaking speed.

Who was she? Why was she teasing him? Was she just a flirt? Why didn't she simply reach out and touch him?

He had to find out.

With perspiration running down his forehead, he did a quick u-turn and gave chase as if his life depended on it.

* * *

Linvall hated it when she dragged him out shopping with her. It could take forever. She was always trying on every dress in the store to see which was the most flattering. Like a lot of women, Marcia was never satisfied with the way she looked. What was the point in the both of them becoming frustrated? She would drag him into a shop and try on a dress and say, "Do you think I'm fat in this?"

He would glance up from studying his copy of the *Racing Post* and look across and ask innocently, "Compared to what?"

If he was lucky, he might see the stiletto heel come flying in his direction at the last moment. Not that it did any good, but at least he wouldn't die of shock as it pierced the corner of his eye.

"We'll start again," she would shout. "Do you think I look fat in this?"

This time he would be concentrating when he answered, "No dear, you look fabulous."

Still, he had no choice but to follow her to the mall after last night.

With little to do but play chaperone to his other half, Linvall's mind soon started wandering . . .

They hadn't been at the shopping mall long when a particularly attractive woman walked past. As it was a hot summer's day, she was wearing a very skimpy tight-fitting little number in electric green which was showing off the perfect curve of her backside and the wiggle in her walk.

No man in his right mind could resist that.

Without him even realising it, Linvall's eyes followed her automatically as men's eyes do when they see a woman they would like to sleep with, even though their woman has warned them of the actual and grievous bodily harm consequences.

Suddenly, a slap came out of nowhere and whacked him in the ear. Hard.

He wanted to scream out with pain, but remembered that he was in public and played it cool. He looked around furtively as his ear burned, making sure that no one had seen.

"Keep the eyes inna your head off that woman," Marcia snapped. She had a vicious look on her face.

"What woman?" Linvall blurted. "I don't see any woman? Oh, you mean this woman? Well, I've never seen her before in my life, have I dear? So would you kindly not flaunt yourself in front of me, because this is my wife over here and she will not take too kindly to it if she sees me trying to sneak a look at your backside when I'm not even noticing it, if you get what I mean. So please get the hell out of here and leave me and my wife to get on with our lives, thank you very much."

The woman looked at him and looked at his wife and

didn't know who to pity more.

"Listen," she said, addressing Linvall, "I've had a bad day, and it usually makes me feel better to see a man smile. I was going to suggest that we lock crotches or that I sit on your face and let you choo-choo-choo, but I wouldn't like to come between you and your woman."

With that she spun on her heels and turned around and disappeared out of his life.

"What did she mean by that?" Linvall cried out.

He turned to Marcia.

"You get some strange people walking through shopping malls nowadays, you know. Care in the community type cases. You think they look pretty and everything, but they're actually basket cases. You get me?"

"You think she's prettier than me, don't you?"

The correct answer was "No" as Linvall very well knew. More elaborately the answer was, "No, of course not dear. You are much prettier." Wrong answers include:

a) "Not prettier, just pretty in a different way."

b) "I don't know how one goes about rating such things."

c) "Yes, but you have a better personality."

d) "Only in the sense that she's younger and thinner."

Like a fool, Linvall opted for over-elaboration, while avoiding the question so that he wouldn't have to lie.

"I swear, Marce, I really wasn't giving her the eye, she just happened to be in my line of vision. What am I supposed to do, close my eyes when she's walking by?"

"That would be a good idea," Marcia suggested.

"But when some hunk of a guy walks past you, you don't close your eyes, do you? You even turn to me for a second opinion."

"That's not the same thing."

"What do you mean it's not the same thing?"

"When I look at another guy I can trust myself to not go and seduce him."

* * *

Even though Johnny had left the ghetto, he had to return there low profile for his food and his barber. He stayed away from Brixton, though, because too many people on that side of town knew him.

He was up in Tottenham, sitting on the barber's leather swing chair, his head tilted back and a clean white napkin around his neck, shaving gel on his face and throat. He had told Fitzroy to give him a shave and to touch the sides and back of his new trademark lowtop fade a little also. As always, Johnny expected nothing but the best from his now regular barber, so there was no need to look in the mirror until the job was done.

Whilst he waited for the haircutting artisan to complete his job, Johnny considered what good fortune he had had in life. What more could he possibly ask for? Well, he could ask to be even richer. He had learned, despite his fabulous wealth, that you could never get enough money. Never. Now he understood how all those big shots like Donald Trump and Richard Branson never ever jacked it in, but kept on going on, even when they had become billionaires. With the cost of living getting dreader and dreader, the rich getting richer and the poor getting poorer, Johnny intended to make sure that he didn't end up poorer. "It is the first duty of every man to be as rich as he possibly can," his father had always told him. "For that you have to make some sacrifices. Nobody ever became the richest man in the world without making sacrifices."

"Last week I made twenty grand with just a couple of phone calls," he boasted to the barber. "Twenty grand — just like that." The click of his fingers emphasised the point. "This week I'm going to make ten grand. Just like that. No problem."

The barber snipped away. "I hope you're going to leave me a big tip, then," he grinned.

Since trimming the locks it had taken him several years to cultivate, Johnny had spent a mini fortune tipping any barber who could camouflage the receding hairline that had been hidden under his mane of natty congo dreads. Despite his wealth, he was still vain. Just the fact that he was living large meant that he didn't even have to look for women, because they usually came looking for him. There was a whole crowd of groupies out there who liked nothing better than a man who didn't think twice about splashing his cash around, and Johnny was always only too happy to oblige whenever he could.

Johnny had only just begun to dreaming of the private island in the Caribbean he would buy someday, when his mobile rang. He reached in his pocket and pulled out his itsy-bitsy model. He flicked it open and answered in his distinctive style, "Yeah-yeah."

It was Linvall, who had been trying to get a hold of him for several days.

"Yeah, I had to change my mobile number," Johnny was explaining. "You know how it go — keeping a low profile."

Linvall explained why keeping a low profile wasn't a bad idea at the moment. Johnny was a wanted man. He told his spar all about Amos.

"What did he want?" Johnny asked.

"That's what I was trying to find out," Linvall replied, "but he wouldn't say. I think some woman is trying to pin a paternity suit on you."

Johnny sighed. Since word had got out about the money he had made and that he was now a millionaire, paternity suits were popping out of the woodwork wherever he turned. He really wished it hadn't gone like that. He wished he could draw back the hands of time and start all over again. Next time, he wouldn't tell a soul that he had become a millionaire because that is where all this gravilicious business started from. He had already been fleeced by one baby mother. He had no intention of spending the rest of his life working for pickney he didn't even know he had.

Good job he had finally got used to using double condoms so there wouldn't be any more mistakes in his life. It had taken him a long time to finally accept that even sucking sweets with the wrapper on could be enjoyable. It wasn't his preferred mode of having sex, but right now it was necessary. Not just for health reasons. With so much money at stake, he simply couldn't afford to be caught out any more. He wasn't about to let some one night stand suddenly present him with a child. No way.

"You sure this detective wasn't the bull man?" he asked Linvall.

"Not unless they've got some really good undercover."

That was music to Johnny's ears.

"If he wasn't the bull, what's there to worry about?" he asked.

"He may not be bull, but it sounds pretty serious to me," Linvall continued. "He's got a list of all your known associates and he intends to pay them all a visit, one by one."

There was a pause down the line.

"So whatcha gonna do?" Linvall asked.

"Stay on the lowdown until I know what's going on. Okay, thanks for the warning, Linvall. Dread out," Johnny said, by way of ending the call. He was going to keep an even lower profile until he could spirit away the bulk of his wealth overseas, beyond the greedy grasp of the CSA.

His visit to the barber's over, Johnny was back in his car. He put the Porsche into gear and headed north. He followed the road out onto the North Circular and then went west to the A1. It was the first real chance he had had to really test the car since he bought it. He pushed hard on the gas pedal and smiled contentedly as the speedometer dial shot up to the hundred mark in seconds. The car handled like a dream on the dual carriageway, taking the road with little vibration of the steering wheel and with hardly a sound coming from the engine. It was at times like this that he felt the power of being successful. He could afford a luxury car now, but he rarely took time out to enjoy it.

He looked in his rearview mirror and realised that he was being flashed down by the car behind. His first thought was that it was the law, and he started to pull over. But it wasn't the law. It was the mystery woman in the same car. She pulled up next to him. There was a big smile on her face as she mouthed the words: 'How would you like to wreck a pum-pum?'

* * *

"You know, I'm having some friends round for dinner. Really big people in the art world, in the TV world, in the world of TV and entertainment. I'd like you to come. You should come round to network if nothing else. On Sunday at my place."

Carmel sounded interested. "I'd love to," came her reply down the phone line.

Gussie woke up early that Sunday morning. He didn't know the first thing about cooking, but he could read and he could use his brain. With a cookbook at hand and with the purchase of some pre-prepared stuff as back-up, he set to work.

He had read somewhere of how a host had impressed a woman with a 12-course dinner where each course was only a morsel in size, but by the end of it the woman had had so many senses and tastes and exotic feelings that she started feeling erotic. Certain foods just turned women on. If only he could concoct some of that magic himself.

She arrived half an hour early, but that didn't matter. He had a chilled glass of white wine at the ready. Handed it to her. She relaxed, admiring his impressive apartment, looking through his CDs, noting down one or two of the selections.

He showed off his trophies. Especially the kung fu ones from the Wushu Academy in Holland. He explained that he had done a year out there on a college scholarship. No, unfortunately, he had not kept up with his martial arts, even though he was getting quite good at the time.

"I still try and keep trim and in shape, though. It helps you work longer I find."

"What kind of 'work' do you mean?" she asked.

"Any kind," he replied, a smile on his face.

He went back to the kitchen.

She relaxed in the convivial atmosphere, kicking back on his sofa. His apartment overlooking the Thames was huge and immaculate.

He heard her call through:

"You know what, you remind me of my ex-boyfriend."

"I won't thank you for that," he replied. "That's probably the most unkind thing anybody's ever said to me."

"Oh, I'm sorry," she said, coming into the kitchen with her drink. "I didn't realise you were so sensitive."

"Only where it hurts. How about you?"

"What?"

"Where are you sensitive."

She smiled. That was a good move.

"That's for you to find out."

"Say the word."

"The word."

He made a move towards her, as if he was just about to kiss her. She pushed him away forcibly.

"Please, you must have me mixed up with some other woman."

That hurt. He recoiled with a whimper.

"So what time is everybody else coming?" she asked.

"They're supposed to be here by now, I don't know what's keeping them. Let's start on the first course anyway. A little okra soup that I made."

Surprisingly, it tasted delicious. He had mixed the okra with evaporated milk and whisked it around a little, added a little flour and, hey presto. Simple but effective, and he probably invented it.

As they ate, they exchanged chit-chat.

"By the way, what sign are you?" he asked.

"Cancer," she replied.

"Oh, so it's your birthday soon."

She smiled. "In a couple of days in fact."

"A couple of days? You'll have to let me take you out."

"Can't I'm afraid, got other plans."

"Pity," he said. And he meant it.

"What sign are you?" she asked.

"Oh, I don't have a star sign," he joked. "But I do have a tree."

Carmel didn't understand.

"Everybody has a tree," Gussie continued. "It's a more accurate measure of who you are. It's a really cool way of knowing yourself, and it's more in line with African astrology."

He reached on the bookshelf and pulled out a book entitled, 'Which Tree Are You?' Carmel flicked through the pages amused:

Which tree did you fall from?
Dec 23 to Dec 31 — Apple Tree
Jan 01 to Jan 11 — Fir Tree
Jan 12 to Jan 24 — Elm Tree
Jan 25 to Feb 03 — Cypress Tree
Feb 04 to Feb 08 — Poplar Tree
Feb 09 to Feb 18 — Cedar Tree
Feb 19 to Feb 28 — Pine Tree
Mar 01 to Mar 10 — Weeping Willow Tree
Mar 11 to Mar 20 — Lime Tree
Mar 21 — Oak Tree
Mar 22 to Mar 31 — Hazelnut Tree
Apr 01 to Apr 10 — Rowan Tree

Apr 11 to Apr 20 — Maple Tree
Apr 21 to Apr 30 — Walnut Tree
May 01 to May 14 — Poplar Tree
May 15 to May 24 — Chestnut Tree
May 25 to Jun 03 — Ash Tree
Jun 04 to Jun 13 — Hornbeam Tree
Jun 14 to Jun 23 — Fig Tree
Jun 24 — Birch Tree
Jun 25 to Jul 04 — Apple Tree
Jul 05 to Jul 14 — Fir Tree
Jul 15 to Jul 25 — Elm Tree
Jul 26 to Aug 04 — Cypress Tree
Aug 05 to Aug 13 — Poplar Tree
Aug 14 to Aug 23 — Cedar Tree
Aug 24 to Sep 02 — Pine Tree
Sep 03 to Sep 12 — Weeping Willow Tree
Sep 13 to Sep 22 — Lime Tree
Sep 23 — Olive Tree
Sep 24 to Oct 03 — Hazelnut Tree
Oct 04 to Oct 13 — Rowan Tree
Oct 14 to Oct 23 — Maple Tree
Oct 24 to Nov 11 — Walnut Tree
Nov 12 to Nov 21 — Chestnut Tree
Nov 22 to Dec 01 — Ash Tree
Dec 02 to Dec 11 — Hornbeam Tree
Dec 12 to Dec 21 — Fig Tree
Dec 22 — Beech Tree

APPLE TREE (the Love) — of slight build, lots of charm, appeal and attraction, pleasant aura, flirtatious, adventurous, sensitive, always in love, wants to love and be loved, faithful and tender partner, very generous, scientific talents, lives for today, a carefree philosopher with imagination.

ASH TREE *(the Ambition) — uncommonly attractive, vivacious, impulsive, demanding, does not care for criticism, ambitious, intelligent, talented, likes to play with fate, can be egotistic, very reliable and trustworthy, faithful and prudent lover, sometimes brains rule over the heart, but takes partnership very seriously.*

BEECH TREE *(the Creative) — has good taste, concerned about looks, materialistic, good organisation of life and career, economical, good leader, takes no unnecessary risks, reasonable, splendid lifetime companion, keen on keeping fit (diets, sports, etc.)*

BIRCH TREE *(the Inspiration) — vivacious, attractive, elegant, friendly, unpretentious, modest, does not like anything in excess, abhors the vulgar, loves life in nature and in calm, not very passionate, full of imagination, little ambition, creates a calm and content atmosphere.*

CEDAR TREE *(the Confidence) — of rare beauty, knows how to adapt, likes luxury, of good health, not in the least shy, tends to look down on others, self-confident, determined, impatient, likes to impress others, many talents, industrious, healthy optimism, waiting for the one true love, able to make quick decisions.*

CHESTNUT TREE (the Honesty) — of unusual beauty, does not want to impress, well-developed sense of justice, vivacious, interested, a born diplomat, but irritates easily and sensitive in company, often due to a lack of self-confidence. Acts sometimes superior, feels not understood, loves only once, has difficulties in finding a partner.

CYPRESS TREE (the Faithfulness) — strong, muscular, adaptable, takes what life has to give, content, optimistic, craves money and acknowledgment, hates loneliness, passionate lover who cannot be satisfied, faithful, quick-tempered, unruly, pedantic, and careless.

ELM TREE (the Noble-mindedness) — pleasant shape, tasteful clothes, modest demands, tends not to forgive mistakes, cheerful, likes to lead but not to obey, honest and faithful partner, likes making decisions for others, noble-minded, generous, good sense of humour, practical.

FIG TREE (the Sensibility) — very strong, a bit self-willed, independent, does not allow contradiction or arguments, loves life, family, children and animals, a bit of a social butterfly, good sense of humour, likes idleness and laziness, of practical talent and intelligence.

FIR TREE (the Mysterious) — extraordinary taste, dignity, sophisticated, loves anything beautiful, moody, stubborn, tends to egoism but cares for those close to them, rather modest, very ambitious, talented, industrious, uncontented lover, many friends, many foes, very reliable.

HAZELNUT TREE (the Extraordinary) — charming, undemanding, very understanding, knows how to make an impression, active fighter for social cause, popular, moody, and capricious lover, honest, and tolerant partner, precise sense of judgment.

HORNBEAM TREE (the Good Taste) — of cool beauty, cares for looks and condition, good taste, is not egoistic, makes life as comfortable as possible, leads a reasonable and disciplined life, looks for kindness and acknowledgement in an emotional partner, dreams of unusual lovers, is seldom happy with feelings, mistrusts most people, is never sure of decisions, very conscientious.

LIME TREE (the Doubt) — accepts what life dishes out in a composed way, hates fighting, stress, and labour, dislikes laziness and idleness. Soft and relenting, makes sacrifices for friends, many talents but not tenacious enough to make them blossom. Often wailing and complaining, very jealous but loyal.

MAPLE TREE (Independence of Mind) — no ordinary person, full of imagination and originality, shy and reserved, ambitious, proud, self-confident, hungers for new experiences, sometimes nervous, has many complexities, good memory, learns easily, complicated love life, wants to impress.

OAK TREE (the Brave) — robust nature, courageous, strong, unrelenting, independent, sensible, does not like change, keeps its feet on the ground, person of action.

OLIVE TREE (the Wisdom) — loves sun, warmth and kind feelings, reasonable, balanced, avoids aggression and violence, tolerant, cheerful, calm, well-developed sense of justice, sensitive, empathetic, free of jealousy, loves to read and the company of sophisticated people.

PINE TREE (the Particular) — loves agreeable company, robust, knows how to make life comfortable, active, natural, good companion, but seldom friendly. Falls easily in love but passion burns out quickly, gives up easily, trustworthy, practical.

POPLAR TREE (the Uncertainty) — looks very decorative, not very self-confident, only courageous if necessary, needs goodwill and pleasant surroundings, very choosy, often lonely, great animosity, artistic nature, good organiser, tends to lean toward philosophy, reliable in any situation, takes partnership seriously.

ROWAN TREE (the Sensitivity) — full of charm, cheerful, gifted without egoism, likes to draw attention. Loves life, motion, unrest, and even complications. Is both dependent and independent, good taste, artistic, passionate, emotional, good company. Does not forgive.

WALNUT TREE (the Passion) — unrelenting, strange and full of contrasts, often egotistic, aggressive, noble, broad horizon, unexpected reactions, spontaneous, unlimited ambition, no flexibility, difficult and uncommon partner, not always liked but often admired, ingenious strategist. Very jealous and passionate. No compromise.

WEEPING WILLOW *(the Melancholy) — beautiful but full of melancholy. Very empathetic, loves anything beautiful and tasteful, loves to travel, dreamer, restless, capricious, honest, can be influenced but is not easy to live with, demanding, good intuition, suffers in love but finds sometimes an anchoring partner.*

As the evening wore on and they were still alone Carmel began to suspect that nobody else was going to show up. Gussie assured her that they were. June Skeets, the TV presenter, Lloyd Carmichael, the young internet millionaire and Henry Bonsu the broadcaster and a few others had phoned to say that they could definitely make it.

Alas, his front door bell didn't ring once.

So it came to the time in the evening, so late in fact that you could almost call it early, when she realised that if she didn't say her farewell, she would fall asleep in his comfy arms.

He suggested that it was no problem, that if she wanted to crash out on the sofa that was all good and well, he had a night shirt she could borrow.

She smiled. All she had to do was say the word, but she wasn't ready for that. Not yet anyway.

It had been a wonderful evening. He had enjoyed himself tremendously despite not even having made a move. He had wanted to, certainly, but just wasn't sure. She hadn't given him the nod and the wink that he needed. He couldn't afford to put a foot wrong with this girl, he didn't want to lose her.

He didn't sleep much that night. She didn't sleep much, either, but he didn't know that. He was thinking of her, and she was thinking of him. She had never met anybody quite like Gussie Braithwaite, certainly not a black man anyway. She wondered whether having a relationship with him would be as much fun as the evening they had spent together. He, meanwhile, was wishing he hadn't tried to impress her so much, or that he hadn't lied about the 'several other homes' he didn't have.

* * *

For that one moment, all the barriers between them fell. It was no longer him or her, it was them. Together in one deep visual embrace. They could hardly wait for that moment seconds later when their arms wrapped warmly around each other in a deep physical embrace.

Beres was still as handsome as she remembered. She took in his steel-grey eyes and muscular body. Her ex-husband was in short sleeves, showing off his toned muscles.

Sonia crossed to the fireplace and stared out of the window.

"You remember that night in the rain?" she asked him. "It was only you and me then."

Beres remembered. He was also in deep contemplation. He fingered his pinstripe moustache and readjusted his gold-rimmed spectacles instinctively. How could he forget that night ten years ago when they first met.

Beres could very well bring up his daughter by himself and, indeed, had done so, but the law saw it differently. Now he had to arrange visiting times with her mother.

He had made his way, as usual, to the huge detached house on Streatham Common which he used to own, but which had ended up in his estranged wife's hands as part of the divorce settlement.

Lara missed her father. He had been there for her ever since she could remember. Been there to encourage her, and always spoiled her. She was, quite simply, his pride and joy.

But Lara was asleep in bed when Beres arrived unexpectedly. Instead, Sonia was there to welcome him.

Gone were the tense vibes. For once, she invited him in instead of sneering at him as he stood on the doorstep. It was the first time he had been in his old house in two years.

"I-I want to explain . . ." she said.

They sat in the living room opposite each other. Staring. Each waiting for the other to speak first. She broke the silence.

"I want there to be no secrets between us."

She told him straight:

"I married you despite knowing that you weren't Mr.

Right. I married on impulse. I was pretty vulnerable at the time and I felt sorry for you. After a lot of soul searching I thought, 'If you're gonna do it, you better do it now.' I imagined that you would be able to make me happy. I was wrong. The marriage was a disaster from the word go, although I didn't realise this until it was all over. My great good fortune was that I fell in love with Grace. I was so needy at the time that I think I would have gone off with the first person who told me I was attractive and showed me affection. It was because of her that I finally left. Once I realised I loved her and that she loved me, it became clear that I had to leave you. I don't remember waking up with the blinding realisation that it was time to go, it was more like a very gradual awareness that there simply wasn't an alternative."

Beres listened. "Why are you telling me all this?" he asked.

"Because Grace told me that you've been snooping around, asking questions, trying to get back together with me again. I just want to get things straight between us. Things that should have been said a long time ago."

Beres sniffed. He should have known that his secret wasn't safe with Grace. Well, he had a few things he wanted to get off his chest as well, a few home truths he wanted Sonia to face. Instead of trying to smooth things over with his ex-wife, he went on the attack, as he had done during those snatched conversations between divorce proceedings.

"I have no regrets about the divorce," he said,

"except that it didn't happen sooner. When I look back on my marriage with you I can't believe what a fool I was to allow myself to stay in that situation. I became the victim in what was a wholly unbalanced relationship. Most importantly, I'm infinitely happier now than I ever was before. I've found the woman I want to spend the rest of my life with, the woman I want to build up a home and start a family with, someone I can place on a pedestal and worship."

She would never forgive him for that outburst. At the time she never said a word. They simply glared at each other with hatred. It was completely spontaneous. Beres realised that he had said something so close to the truth, that it probably was true, only he didn't realise how true it was until he said it

In truth, divorce was a great blight on Beres's life. He took it bad. Before it happened he had reached a point where at last he was earning enough money to provide well for his family, then suddenly it was over. He didn't know how to handle the situation. He felt it would be years before he'd be reasonable company for another human being.

Things weren't really right again until he met Caroline, and even then it was difficult. It seemed as if she would, quite understandably, always resent the way their relationship had begun but, miraculously, everything seemed suddenly to fit into place and he managed to put all the horror behind him and start again.

The divorce still felt painful, but Beres tried not to

brood on it too much. It's too easy, as a divorced man living away from your child, to buy into self-pity. Towards the end of their seven-year marriage, all he could think about was keeping his wife sweet. He didn't stop to consider that she felt she could do exactly as she pleased. By the end she was treating him as if he was someone the cat had brought home.

It wouldn't have been as bad if she had had an affair with another man, he could live with that, but going off with another woman was like telling him that he didn't suffice as a man. Somewhere deep inside of him, he wanted just one more opportunity to prove to Sonia that he was a real man. One hundred percent Caribbean man!

* * *

Gussie called Carmel early the next evening. Despite Yemi's reluctance to give him any information on Carmel, he had figured out her SP for himself. The penny had finally dropped. He had had to scramble amongst his old copies of *The Voice* newspaper to find what he was looking for. There it was in black and white, a feature on young black artist Carmel De Souza, the daughter of the late J. Arthur De Souza. J. Arthur De Souza! The multi-millionaire.

Carmel De Souza was born an heiress, and raised that way. As a child, her governess was under strict instructions not to allow her near the kitchen or to do anything else that would get her delicate hands dirty.

Her father had made his money in finance, and eventually became Britain's richest black man. Gussie remembered reading about the millionaire lifestyle, the huge yacht and homes in New York, the South of France and Compass Point in the Bahamas. He also had a penthouse on Park Lane and a house in Holland Park, where he lived with his wife and two beautiful daughters.

Now that he knew who she was, Beres was more than keen to see Carmel again. But the first thing she explained when she picked up the phone was that she was in a rush and wondering if she was going to make it to the theatre in time. She was meeting somebody in the foyer. A man, it turned out. They were going to see some romantic comedy.

"Maybe some other time."

"Yeah, maybe some other time," Gussie said.

He might have known that she was all tied up. A woman this good doesn't stay single long enough for a man like him to casually pass by and pluck her up.

The only thing Gussie could do was hope and pray.

"If you ever need me to sit again, just call. I really enjoyed myself," he offered.

"Yeah, sure."

"No, I really mean it. Hey, we're practically neighbours. You're welcome to pass by any time you want."

"I wish I could say the same," she said, "but I'm always so busy with one thing or another, that it's not always convenient. But, yeah, I'll call you."

That was good enough for Gussie.

For now.

He replaced the handset in its cradle. He had to see this woman again, and soon.

Carmel De Souza had just ten minutes to get to the South Bank. She gunned the throttle of her Kawasaki Ninja 600 and lurched forward on the back wheel, leaving the cars standing at the traffic lights. She stole a glance into her rearview mirror with a satisfied grin. That would teach them to not allow her the space she needed to overtake. She squeezed the throttle some more, her eyes darting from left to right, her mind aware that at any moment a car could pull out without indicating, and cause her to take a tumble. For her, car drivers were the only negative thing about riding a powerful bike in London.

It took no time at all to cover the couple of miles to the arts complex on the south side of the River Thames. In fact, she had a few minutes to spare as she parked the Ninja up on a pavement, climbed off, removed her helmet, unzipped her leather jumpsuit to reveal jeans and a loose sweater, locked up the bike and set the alarm. Carrying the helmet with her, she made her way to the Lyttleton Theatre for the opening night of a new production of *Othello* on the South Bank.

Ben was waiting for her in the foyer, frantically pacing up and down. He looked relieved to eventually see her.

"Thank goodness you've arrived. I thought you were not going to make it. They're refusing to allow people in once the curtain goes up."

"Oh Ben, you are such a worrier sometimes. Have I ever been late yet?"

There was no time to discuss the matter. The last call for the theatregoers to take their seats had rung.

* * *

She was dressed in a rather fetching 'Shirley Bassey' glittering evening gown which thrust her breasts up in such a way that even the most disinterested man would immediately get an eyeful of the good stuff that made women famous. She looked stunning with more than a little touch of class about her.

"Hey, big boy, is that a rocket in your pocket, or are you just happy to see me?"

If he wasn't stiff already, Johnny certainly was when the woman came up and gave him a friendly pat between the legs.

He had only had a drink or two at the hotel bar, drowning his sorrows in deep thought, wondering how long he would have to keep a low profile away from his usual haunts. Apart from the well-established, old school gigolos with one or two wealthy 'friends' who kept them in Armanis, the bar was filled with freelance chancers who cruise rich women and male escorts waiting for their sex date.

"Can I get you a drink?" he offered, as the woman rummaged half-heartedly in her purse.

She looked at him briefly for a moment, considering

the proposition and smiled.

"You don't have to buy me a drink," she said, "let's just go straight over to your place now."

Even though he felt and walked like a jockey who'd been riding his donkey all day, Johnny was only too happy to add one more notch to his belt. He took the woman by the arm and led her to the service apartment he was renting on Curzon Street, just a few minutes away.

You see, Mayfair was the last place anyone would think of looking for him, Johnny had decided. He had the money to rent a penthouse in the area for a few weeks, no problem.

Her name was Cynthia, and she claimed that she didn't usually do this kind of thing, but the booze had been doing the talking for her.

"Absolutely fabulous place you've got here," she said. "You don't know how lucky you are."

"Oh yes I do," said Johnny mysteriously. "I'm able to go out and meet charming women like yourself and invite them back and they are always suitably impressed. I know I am very lucky in some respects."

Cynthia smiled. She liked men who came straight to the point. She caressed the back of his neck with a warm hand.

"I don't know what it is," she whispered in his ear, "you're so nice, so nice."

Johnny reciprocated with flattering words about her, too.

"So," she said with an air of finality, "are you ready

to go to bed?"

Johnny's smile left no doubt as to the answer. He could think of nothing better. Somehow he managed to play it cool.

"Yeah, why not," he said, shrugging his shoulders.

Cynthia got up and took his hand. She let him lead her into the master bedroom with its king size four-poster bed in the middle.

"Make yourself comfortable, I'll just be a minute," she said, pausing long enough before disappearing into the en suite bathroom

Johnny didn't waste any time. He pulled his shirt off his back as fast as he could, losing a couple of buttons in the process, then it was off with his trousers quickly, stumbling slightly with them snagged around his ankles. He hopped on one foot onto the bed before eventually succeeding in flinging the troublesome trousers across the room. He lay there naked on the perfumed duvet, on his back looking up at the ceiling, his fingers wandering over the soft silk sheets to the walnut headboard.

"Young rich and single is the way to be," Johnny found himself humming as Cynthia returned from the bathroom wearing nothing but a thong around her waist.

"So, do you want me to stay the night?" she asked him.

Johnny nodded his head greedily.

"Then that will be £800," she said. "In advance."

* * *

Thanks to the Ninja, Carmel made it home about twenty minutes before Ben's new registration Aston Martin pulled up outside her building. It was just enough time for her to jump in the shower. That was another thing about riding around in leathers, she always felt so sweaty afterwards.

She turned on the cold shower as she always did whenever she was in an erotic mood and gasped as the initial jet hit her skin. She hadn't realised what a sexy writer Shakespeare was until tonight's sensuous production of *Othello*. The performance had inspired her with an idea for a nude painting featuring Othello and Desdemona as he accuses her of being unfaithful. She could see it now.

The buzzer went just as she was growing accustomed to the water temperature and she climbed out of the shower to buzz Ben in. A couple of minutes later, he entered her apartment panting heavily.

"You really need to move to somewhere with a lift," he puffed. "Either that, or swap apartments with the bloke on the ground floor."

"You mean, you need to get yourself fit," she said with a glint in her eye. She pulled him towards her by his necktie. "I've got just what the doctor ordered — a good workout."

He smiled too, pulled her towards him, her wet breasts against his white shirt.

"You're cold," he said.

"Freezing," she replied. "But you can warm me up."

"I have your permission?"

"You have my command."

"In that case, let me start here," he said.

Deftly, Ben lifted her up by the waist with his powerful arms until her crotch was level with his nose, then with her legs on his shoulders and his tongue pointed upwards, he went to work.

In this manner he carried her towards the bedroom area. After laying her down gently on the brass bed, he continued darting around with his tongue, using his whole mouth, sucking and pulling gently with his teeth and bringing his fingers into play.

What Ben lacked in the missionary position, he more than made up for when he went downtown. It always amazed Carmel that a man who was otherwise so conservative and unimaginative in bed, could be so devastatingly adept orally.

She could have come two or three times more if she wanted to. But as her first gasps of ecstacy died down, it was replaced by a steady drone at the foot of the bed.

He was asleep!

She couldn't believe it. He really was asleep. She tapped him gently but insistently on the top of his head with her foot, which startled him.

"Wh-what?"

"You fell asleep."

"Oh, sorry, I've been so busy at work this week, I'm absolutely shattered."

"What's new."

"No, really, this week has been worse than ever. And I'm flying overseas tomorrow . . ."

Ben had discussed his internet start-up with Carmel before deciding to set up the company. He had explained that it would mean a lot of hard work, long hours and travelling. She had insisted that he should do whatever he desired. But, of late, there hadn't been much of a relationship to talk about. She hadn't realised that doing whatever Ben desired would mean only seeing each other once a month.

She reached over to her bedside table for a cigarette and lit it, just because she knew that Ben didn't like it.

He started coughing as if he was going to die.

"Must you?" he asked.

"If you're falling asleep, I might as well. So you're not going to be around for my birthday."

"Well, I won't be around for the next five weeks actually. That's why I wanted to make this evening so nice," he explained, "because it's going to be our last for a while."

"Go on."

"Well, it's just that it's so much easier to raise venture capital in the States. I'm flying out there in a couple of days to meet all the real big money men."

Carmel sighed. She wasn't interested. In fact, she was glad of it. With Ben's tongue at a safe distance she would be able to re-evaluate their relationship and consider whether she wanted it to continue on these terms or whether she was better off fishing in some other sea.

When she thought about it, little more had kept her in that relationship over the last six months than the fact that Ben was only a heartbeat away from being heir to a vast estate in Northumberland, not to talk of a hacienda covering a hundred thousand acres of Argentinian pampas, which had belonged to his family for a hundred years and on which a quarter of a million head of cattle roamed. More importantly, Ben was heir to a title. He reckoned that it wouldn't take long for his elderly uncle to pop off, and as uncle had no natural heirs of his own Ben stood to become a very rich man indeed. Not to talk of that dukedom. But it had been two years now, and his uncle seemed determined to outlive his nephew. So, while he was waiting in vain, Ben occupied himself with trying to become rich quick through the internet.

Of the many boyfriends that Carmen had had over the years, Ben would not have been her number one choice. But like her mother, and her mother before that, Carmen had been taught the wisdom of marrying money.

Like many of her female contemporaries, Carmel had gambled that she didn't need to settle down young. She considered that to be old fashioned. In her view, science allowed the modern woman to fit marriage and children in with her lifestyle. Carmel believed that she could afford to enjoy herself and pick and choose the best of the crop, at least until she was in her thirties.

She was in her thirties now, and Ben was her insurance policy.

Oh, she knew what she was worth, and her mother was always reminding her of it. She was Carmel De Souza, daughter of the late J. Arthur. If her father hadn't left all his wealth to his twenty-four year old mistress and their love child, they might have been one of the richest black families in the country. Instead, they were 'also rans' doing an excellent job of keeping up appearances.

"Don't let the family down. It's your duty to marry for richer and not poorer," her mother never tired of reminding her. "You don't even have to love your husband. I never once loved your father, but that didn't stop me from marrying him and giving birth to his children."

Even Carmel's younger sister, Amy, had married a Swedish porn millionaire, who was well-off enough to install his wife into a huge mansion standing in its own grounds in Edgware, where Amy had to do little more than give instructions to their Filipino maids, English gardeners and French cook.

"When I get back from the States, why don't we go away for a holiday? My treat," Ben said.

Carmel turned to him and smiled.

"Yeah, that would be nice. I've always wanted to go on a cruise to the Bahamas," she suggested.

Ben nodded and decided to change the subject by resuming where he had left off — crotchwise and otherwise.

The fire had, however, fizzled out. The desire Carmel had felt a few minutes earlier, was all but extinguished.

Now, she wanted her place to herself. She wanted to light a few candles, and sit and meditate. She needed to be alone when she did that, or at least not have Ben there. He never took anything like that seriously. Said she was wasting her time, because he was Mister Be Real, and didn't believe in anything that he couldn't reduce to a workable mathematical formula.

* * *

Gussie was up early the next morning and round at Carmel's building by eight with a magnum bottle of champagne. A man only gets one shot in his lifetime to meet a woman like Carmel De Souza, he decided, and he intended to make the most of his opportunity.

The entryphone exploded in a babble of garbled syllables.

"Who is it?" A man's voice.

"It's Gus."

"Who?"

"Gus!"

He was buzzed in immediately.

The tall and bulky figure of Ben greeted him at the door to Carmel's apartment, dressed in only a night gown.

"Who are you?" Ben grunted, wiping the sleep from his eyes.

"I'm Gus."

"Gus, I thought you said you were 'post'."

Ben made to close the door. Gussie only just

managed to stick his foot in the way.

"Is Carmel not around?" he asked.

"No," Ben replied simply, his eyes fixed on the giant bottle of champagne. He had seen the label and knew it was the good stuff.

"It's her birthday today," Gussie said, holding up the champagne by way of explanation.

"Yes, I know."

"Could you see that she gets this when she gets back — from Gussie."

Gussie handed him the bottle and was just about to turn when a lightbulb seemed to light in Ben's head.

"Gussie? You're that bloke aren't you? I thought I recognised you."

Gussie stretched out his hand, but Ben left it hanging in thin air.

"I've heard about you, you're the one who can't keep your snozzle under control. Yemi told me you might be lurking about. I hope you're not coming round here with any ideas. Carmel is my woman. You understand?"

"Yeah, yeah, yeah. No worries. Just make sure she gets the bubbly."

Gussie nodded a half-hearted farewell and departed, wondering what Carmel was doing with an idiot.

That was basically the same thing that Carmel was thinking as she jogged another circuit around Victoria Park. Thirty years old today, she was in absolutely no hurry to find a man, but life kept reminding her that she was THIRTY. Not just life, either. But her mother, who had invested so much in her over the years, had phoned up at seven in the morning to inform her daughter that, for every year, her investment was losing value.

That's the kind of woman Millicent De Souza was. Everything was pounds, shillings and pence to her. It wasn't a question of whether she liked Ben or not, it was a question of how much longer he was going to keep her daughter hanging on a string while he twiddled his thumbs deciding whether to marry or not. She couldn't abide by that. As far as she could see, Ben should be glad to have a woman like her daughter for a wife.

Carmel looked at her watch. She had been running for nearly an hour. Her early morning jogs were the secret behind her tight, flat stomach and her general tip-top shape. Puffing lightly, she made her way out of the park to jog the last half mile home down the Hackney Road.

When she got back to her flat, Ben had already left. To her delight she found the magnum of champagne on the kitchen table with a card from him saying simply:

Darling, for you, on your birthday.

* * *

It wasn't until morning that Johnny Dollar finally stepped out of the hotel. It had been a wicked session. He had been at it all night. He didn't even know that a woman could be that good, indeed he hadn't even known that he could be that good. Even at the time when he was most exhausted, he just seemed to carry on. When a woman's that good, no matter how it hurts you just keep on giving it up and enjoying the mixture of pain and pleasure/sweet and sour without complaining.

But you can't keep making love in a hotel room for ever. However long you stay undercover, at some time you've got to come up for air, or at least to do some shopping.

Johnny had been holed up in the hotel for weeks, doing little else than watching videos all day long, then sneaking out under cover of darkness, to go and find himself a woman. But on this particular Sunday afternoon, he was dying for hunger. And not just any hunger, but for some nice jerk chicken, made the way mamma used to make it.

He had decided to avoid Brixton, though, and had driven East to Hackney, to a nice little Caribbean takeaway place that he was familiar with at Clapton Pond.

It was a near-fatal mistake.

No sooner had he climbed out of his car than he heard a familiar woman's voice cry out, "Is that you Johnny Dollar?"

Johnny turned round to greet Lesley's mum.

"So what happen, Mrs. P?" he said.

Had he remembered Lesley's mum's warning after the last time, of what she would do to him with a meat cleaver should she find out that he had had a baby again with a woman other than her daughter, he would have climbed back in that car and driven away fast. But he had forgotten all about that, and thought everything was just fine and dandy between him and her.

Fortunately for Johnny, Mrs. P didn't have a meat cleaver to hand at that precise moment, but her umbrella proved to be an equally deadly weapon. Like a knight in shining armour taking part in a jousting contest she charged him as fast as her legs could carry her, the sharp tip of her umbrella aimed at the area between his legs.

With his back against the wall, it seemed like Johnny's days of jumping from one woman's bed to another were over for good. There was nowhere to run, nowhere to hide, and from the look in Mrs. P's eyes, she wasn't about to take "No, please don't, not my balls!" for an answer.

Suddenly, out of nowhere, there was a screech of tyres as Suzuki Vitara raced around the corner. As it neared Johnny, it mounted the pavement, and the passenger door flew open and a voice shouted, "Quick, jump in!"

Johnny didn't need to be asked twice. He threw himself into the jeep and, as it sped away, he could see Mrs. P in the rearview mirror, waving her umbrella in the air, as if she was saying 'I'll be back'.

"Hey man, I don't know how to thank you. I really don't," Johnny gasped, observing his saviour for the first time.

The burly black man looked to be in his late forties, it was hard to tell. He had a big grin on his face. His face looked strangely familiar, but Johnny couldn't pinpoint it. He was just glad that the brotha happened to be there when he needed him most.

"No problem," he said. "My name is Amos, Amos Butler. As a matter of fact, I've been looking for you, Johnny. The voices in my head told me to come get you and reason with you. With my words of wisdom you'll soon be able to add the word 'man' after your surname."

* * *

Linvall was the proudest father in the world as he sat down at home on the couch and listened to the 'big showdown' on the radio between his thirteen-year-old son Lacquan, aka DJ Pickney, the 'baddest' reggae mc in the land, and the older Trigga Ranks, both of whom had been engaged in a vinyl for vinyl counteraction with each other for the last six months. It was the most talked about clash in reggae music, with each artist becoming more and more insulting to the other on their 'answer back' records. In particular, Trigga Ranks was vexed that DJ Pickney had made a record in which he hinted in the coded messages of bad bwoy slang that the older mc's sexual orientation was open to debate. Most of the record buying public were calling for an end to the counteraction, but little did they know that the management of both artists were very keen for it to continue as record sales for the two entertainers had soared beyond everyone's wildest expectations, and reggae music (which had been languishing in the doldrums for several years) was now, once again, booming up the charts. In a strange way, the rivalry between the two had produced each artist's best lyrics.

The showdown was taking place on Ruffneck FM, the adjudicator was popular radio disc jockey David Honeyghan who, though hailing from Newcastle, could do a bloody good impersonation of a Jamaican deejay.

"First things first," Honeyghan began. "DJ Pickney, how old are you exactly."

"Just turn thirteen, y'know Honey," Pickney said in a thick patois which he always assumed for showbiz purposes.

"Thirteen?!" Honeyghan sounded impressed. "From your voice I expected somebody older."

"Everybody say that my voice bigger than me," Lacquan replied. "Me really born with that voice, and from the start it's been that way, me never really sit down and develop it."

HONEYGHAN: So when did the counteraction really start?

TRIGGA: Well, Honey, it really start when D.J. Pickney do dat record where him seh 'In the wild wild West, dem man with trigga love to ride 'arse' . . .

PICKNEY: Me nevah seh 'arse' me seh 'horse'. Horse is arse an arse is horse when you chat Jamaican. You want me to say 'hoarse' like Englishman? Jamaican language is Jamaican language, English is English. Why you ah try to turn around words, Trigga?

TRIGGA: (raising his voice) H-o-r-s-e isn't that a horse? An' a-r-s-e isn't that an arse-hole? Everybody know seh you is a literate yout'. Explain yourself, man.

PICKNEY: Me nevah seh dat. Me seh, 'Him ride horse inna West'. Batty man tek me argument and get vexed.

TRIGGA: Me nuh tek dem t'ings, me is a Gemini man, mek me tell you dat. You is a man dat go round and talk and t'row your talk and then when you see me you smile. Me nuh tek dat you know, bwoy. Me is a one a way yout. Ah nuh your friend dem deh see me down the road and seh me ah gay?

PICKNEY: Which one ah my friend dem?

TRIGGA: All ah your friends dem.

PICKNEY: Which part dem see you?

TRIGGA: Everywhere.

PICKNEY: Trigga, mek me ask you somet'ing. Man say a man a gay an' you know you nuh gay, how dat fe offend you?

TRIGGA: Honey, mek me ask you a question . . . You a big man an' ah go down the road an' a man see you from out ah blues and come out and seh 'faggot Honey', dat nuh go offend you, my yout'?

HONEYGHAN: Well, bwoy, I'm telling you, I don't like to hear dat name. It's a form of disrespect, you haffe understand yout'.

TRIGGA: Ah dat me ah show yuh. Every man fe know wha' him ah do. Don't gimme no excuse, me no tek alibi. You can't call me a faggot, dem t'ings nuh right, y'know. Dat is not counteraction.

PICKNEY: Me nuh counteract you, me retaliate. Let me tell you the whole bottom line, Honey. Me know dem man since me was a yout, seen? And sometimes we just deh-deh and chat some lyrics, seen? All type of lyrics: Cock up your batty and ride, when you see your matey and she don't look right. Seen? From that, me build my own t'ing — Love up your woman dem right, if you wanna stop all the fussing and fight. Put my lyrics together. Tune voice, tune come ah road, tune start sell. Seen? Then all on a sudden dis talk is about, dat me come offa Trigga's style.

TRIGGA: Ah nuh so?

PICKNEY: No, man.

TRIGGA: My yout' yuh a liad deh so, man, you ah liad deh so. Is a lie you ah tell.

PICKNEY: Every deejay in this business, me talk about EVERY deejay, seen — Shabba Ranking, Bounty Killa, Beenie Man — all the great deejay, they all come offa people's style an' people's t'ings, seen? Ah Buju Banton sing Big it up — gal in ah your batty rider, murder — you must fe waan the deejay chat for . . . And then you come with your style offa it: Rip it up- 'member me seh it get ruff, hear dis, man ah chat so much lyrics an' stuff . . . Me an' you are in the same camp, Trigga.

TRIGGA: Yout', yuh must waan fe get expelled from school — I am the headmaster so siddung and tek rule, seen? Yuh out deh ah push your luck, but yuh can't gwan . . . If a war you a look for, wish you all de best still.

HONEYGHAN: Gentlemen, we need to find a solution to end this counteraction. What kind of solution do you think would end all of this?

TRIGGA: Ah who start it fe end it, y'know, Honey. A solution can't just come so. You have to do it from your heart. It reach the point where either you done with it, or you ah go keep forward with it.

PICKNEY: You seh me start it.

HONEYGHAN: Let's forget ah who start it, let's put that aside. The damage done do already, so it's up to the two man dem to mek a solution to the problem.

PICKNEY: Me a big man, seen, but no disrespect to any man. Trigga is more than a friend. He's a man wha' mek me see how certain t'ings ah gwan inna the reggae industry. He is a man whe' put down certain t'ings wha' me pick up, who mek me know meself. So me offend you, Trigga? You shouldn't feel offended.

TRIGGA: Dem t'ing deh nuh call for. Me would ah like to see us forget everyt'ing wha'ppen between the two of us and start something new, y'know, start anew. Because it can't continue like this. From him seh it done it done. If a man start something him haffe finish it. You get it? If him nevah do not'n 'gainst me, me nevah do not'n 'gainst him. Y'know dat. Why him tell me how I ah ride horse, what is a horse. Nuh him first call me gay, then? Check it out. Why it nevah connect?

HONEYGHAN: Yuh see you two deejays now, you should be role models for all the yout' dem, you should really set a standard. The two of you must come together.

PICKNEY: Okay me ah go mek the first step: ME DONE WITH ALL AH DAT. SEEN? Me ah go stop it because it ah irritate me . . .

Linvall didn't get to hear any more of the programme, because at that very moment, Marcia stormed in.

"I've just had a call from Mrs. Dutta?"

"Mrs. Dutta?"

"You know, the headmistress at Lacquan's school. She doesn't know where he is, he hasn't been at school all week, he's been bunking off. She's had enough, and she's decided to exclude him from school."

Quickly, but slyly, Linvall reached for the volume control of the radio and turned it down. This was the wrong time to admit that he knew exactly where D.J. Pickney was. He hadn't even thought for a moment that Lacquan had to be cutting school if he was on air in the middle of the afternoon.

"What's she talking about excluding him," he said with more bravado, "you mean expelling him?"

"Exclude, expel, call it what you will. It adds up to the same thing: Lacquan's life is ruined, and all because of you."

"Hold on, hold on. First things first. First, she can't just exclude him like that. If he hasn't been attending school she should have told us. Anyway, what do you mean, it's all my fault?"

"Of course it's all your fault. There isn't a day that goes by that I don't think of what I went through on my own all those years. If you had been a responsible father from the day your child was born, none of this would have happened."

Linvall sighed. He didn't want to go down that road. It was an argument he couldn't win, even though it wasn't all his fault. But when it came to raising children, no matter what the father did and how the mother made him suffer, the woman was always right.

"Look, calm down. Let me call this Mrs. Dutta and arrange for us to go up to Brixton High as soon as possible to discuss matters."

* * *

"So, Johnny Dollar, you know how much people ah look fe you?"
"Which people?"
"Well, your baby mother for a start. I'm afraid I'm going to have to take you in, idren. This is the end of the line. You've been in this baby fathering thing long enough, spreading your seed here and there and not caring about the consequences. Every thing comes to an end some day, it happens to us all and this is the end for you."
Johnny still couldn't believe what he was hearing
"Is this some kind of a joke?"
"Well, you might find it funny, but I'm afraid that the rest of the nation doesn't find it amusing to have to pay for your pickney dem."
"But I pay for my pickney."
"Not this one you don't . . ."

Johnny stared at the photo Amos had pulled out of his breast pocket. It was of a young ghetto boy of eight or nine or ten. The boy looked familiar, but like who?

"Look closely," Amos said, "are you sure you don't recognise the boy?"

Johnny shook his head. No. Definitely not.

"Are you sure you don't see yourself when you look into his eyes?" Amos pressed on.

Johnny was surprised at the suggestion. "Of course not," he replied. The boy looked more like one of his friends than him. Linvall possibly, or Beres, but definitely not him. He couldn't see himself in the boy at all.

"So what is all this about?" Johnny asked finally.

"I could ask you the same question," Amos replied. "Anybody in the world can see that that is your pickney, no doubt about it."

Johnny continued denying, denying and denying.He explained to Amos, trying to make the detective see reason, "Ever since I've struck rich, all these avaricious women have come out of the woodwork claiming that I am the father to their child. I can't possibly be the father to all the fatherless children in the world, can I? It stands to reason. Don't you see, it's a conspiracy. The women out there are determined to distress me, just because I'm a successful black man who likes to put himself about a bit. I'm innocent. Innocent. You get me? You tell all those women to find some other mug to fleece, because my money ain't going to keeping their pickney in shoes and pants. You get me? Women are always saying, 'How come black men are so tight with their money? One thing that a lot of these women have to learn is that a black man isn't made of money."

"I suspect that the man doth protest too much," Amos said. "Take your mind back some ten years ago. Don't you remember Verna?"

"Verna? Who's that?"

"Have you forgotten? The girl with the long hair extensions done perfectly into a beehive, not a hair out of place. Young-looking, when you met she was wearing a shiny, glittery number on top with a skirt that matched and, ooooh, she looked good enough to eat, so you decided to pluck up the courage to check her?"

It was starting to come flooding back to Johnny. He remembered that evening. He didn't know what it was, despite all his reservations and unwillingness to be made a fool of in front of all her friends, he felt he had to get over there and talk to her. Before you could say 'Rewind, selector!' he found himself sliding expertly across the bar as if he was a professional lounge lizard, and telling her so earnestly 'Are you religious? 'Cause I'm the answer to all your prayers!"

At first she was reluctant. She wasn't even attracted to him. But she felt sorry for him, took pity on him, even when her friends were suggesting that she should diss him bad.

He interpreted her indifference as playing hard to get. But he was too cute for her to resist. Especially when he started dropping lines like: 'Do you sleep on your front? Do you mind if I do?'

She smiled at him, but failed to make eye contact. Not because she had difficulty in looking a man directly in the eyes, nor necessarily due to shyness, but because her eyes were not located in her chest.

Johnny was too sober to fall in love. He found her interesting, because she allowed him to do all the talking. He wanted to kiss her, desired her touch, longed for a glance from her eyes. Yet he was confusing 'attraction', with sexual hunger. Far from love at first sight, he was just extremely horny and not entirely choosy about the women he met.

As far as Johnny was concerned, she could keep her

beauty, intelligence, charisma. All he was interested in was putting a lash on her. And as long as she didn't want more to the relationship with him than just intercourse, a lash was what he was going to put on her. In his view, every woman was easy and had the sexual morals of a man. Even though certain prigs pretended that they wanted to stay virgins until married, his experience had taught him that women were no different from men — they just said they were. He had even met one or two women who had wanted sex more than he did.

"Remember what the bedroom was like?" Amos continued jogging Johnny's memory.

How could he forget. Custom built for pum-pum with mirrors on the ceiling, a bed filled with five hundred gallons of water — ideal for the motion of sex. She told him that no man had yet lain on it who didn't go absolutely crazy and wild for it. He could see why.

She pulled back gleaming white sheets, newly-laundered. He could hardly wait, the whiteness was like an invitation to come on down. And that's what he did.

They fell on the bed and rolled around in a tight embrace. He stripped naked once the lights were out and hid under the blankets. She joined him, keeping her bra and panties on.

"Of course I'll respect you in the morning," he promised her. "No, of course I'm not sleeping with anyone else."

He had been taught by the best. Older women who were always willing to give the young prodigy a lesson or two in love. It had started when he was just a schoolboy. Housewives with penchants for teenage bubas had grabbed his, the moment they got a chance and had taught him how to make good use of it to satisfy a woman. He had been a keen student and went on from there, graduating with forty year old women, and older still, by the time he was eighteen.

And talk about keeping his promises. His regular diet of okra soup, irish moss and mannish water kicked in. Every time he drank that combination, he was dangerous.

Any girl that got the sweetness from Johnny during that period was bound to get the full lashing of love potion number nine. No two ways about it. He didn't need to bathe her in nice scented oils and massage her down to put her in the mood for some kiss or grind, all she had to do was kick back, drink some wine and feel fine.

You couldn't even call it a one night stand really. He had simply been servicing her because her boyfriend (an old school mate of Johnny's) was spending the night with his other girlfriend, leaving Verna in bed alone and so pissed off she wanted revenge. What better way to do it. Though it was some time ago, Johnny remembered that she had told him that she was on the pill. He hadn't even thought twice about it. They just did it, for virtually twenty-four hours. They started some time in the afternoon and went on all night. By midday the next day, he was the one crying out for mercy, saying "No more, no more, no more!" But Verna was, as yet, not satisfied. She simply went into her freezer and pulled out a tub of Haagen Dazs and fed it to him. Before he knew it, he was ready to go again. In fact, during that session, Verna taught him a thing or two about sex that he didn't previously know. She allowed him to infiltrate the inner passageways of her heart and there inside he saw the rhythm of her life, longing to be in sync with his. He had hardly pushed the tip of his manhood in again when he came in convulsions.

"Aaaaaaaaaaaahhh, that's right," he gasped.

She pushed him off and rolled over.

"You came too soon!" she groaned.

Put it this way, it was one of the great sexual adventures in his life. She had to grab on to anything she could hang on to. With her legs on his shoulders, they did it in the kitchen, the hall and in the bathroom. She started to bawl, "Laaaaaaawd woy!"

The boy clearly done good. Johnny was so sweet, he made Verna feel like strawberries were his favourite treat. He was the best lover she had ever had. He could suck, lick and grind. He had taken her to the very edge of her sexual imagination and then make her beg. She showed her appreciation by freaking out. By the time the session was coming to an end, Johnny knew the veggie was all his — bought, hoodwinked and bamboozled.

"Okay, you may come now," he told her finally.

Her voice seemed to shake with the words, "Thank you, thank yooouuuohmigodooooouh-uh-uh-uh. Uhhhhh!"

In a panic afterwards, Verna started clearing up and hunting for any signs of Johnny's hair on the sheets, and any other evidence of Johnny having been there.

He left her house something of a master in the art of sex.

The next time he went round there, she was telling him that she had bought a pack of three and that it would be such a waste not to use them.

Johnny took one look at her and decided, 'No, no, no, I can't do it, she'll only want to create this scene on a regular basis.' He had got his oats and, already, Verna was beginning to look less appetising. Now, those endearing little qualities that initially attracted him to her seemed to irritate him. He no longer saw pouting lips, but a scowl on her face. That little giggle that she had, now sounded to Johnny like a cackle.

"So is that it?" she asked. "Won't you let me at least have my satisfaction once more?"

He said he had a headache.

She couldn't believe that he thought so little of her that he couldn't even be bothered to come up with a better excuse. She couldn't believe that she was getting played like this.

Johnny was saved by the bell or, rather, the buzz on the door. Verna jumped up. She threw him his underpants and made him grab the rest of his clothes and hide under the bed. But it was a false alarm. The minicab driver had got the wrong address.

Imagine his surprise, weeks later, while lying in bed at home with Lesley on his arm one night, Verna calls him up all the way from the States to tell him she's pregnant and that he's the dad. Johnny thought it was a joke at first, and wasn't going to stand for it. A poor joke by all accounts.

Amos smiled as he drove. He could almost hear Johnny thinking.

"Have you never wondered what happened after that one night when you and Verna got it on?" Amos asked.

Johnny didn't need to wonder. Verna had waged a postal assault on him. He had humoured her to begin with, and exchanged correspondence for a while. He had tried to reason with her that it was just a one night stand. Then he had to get cruel.

"In case you don't remember that part, let me remind you," said Amos as he swung onto the Eastway heading south. "You abandoned her, left her stranded and she even resorted to drinking to overcome her own feelings of mistrust, anger, betrayal. When she announced she was pregnant, you begged her to have an abortion."

"Abortion?" Johnny couldn't believe what he was hearing.

"All she wanted," Amos continued, "was a relationship, a commitment, a faithful boyfriend, a best friend to confide in. But now she wants diamonds and more diamonds. Hard cash. An extremely expensive car. She only drives cars made in Italy with the names of the manufacturer ending with 'i'. Hope I covered everything."

"I think you have things a little confused," Johnny

told him. He didn't even know for sure that he had got her pregnant. Sure, she had said so, but he thought she was only joking, her way of duping him into a relationship. How could she have got pregnant if they were using protection?

He had told her to be serious, but she hadn't listened to him. She just kept on insisting that she was going to have the child and that she wouldn't ask for anything from him, that she could bring up the child on its own, that he was never going to see the child and so on.

"People don't joke about dem kinda t'ings," he warned her in a veiled whisper.

She insisted that she wasn't joking.

"It's no big deal," she said, "I'm going to go ahead and have the kid, but you've got nothing to worry about. I'll look after him or her myself."

She had ended up being so ignorant, that he fell out with her bad. She cussed his mother in a letter. He wasn't about to allow that. She could have sooner cussed his father, sister — anybody, but not his mother. From that moment on he didn't want to have anything to do with her. That was the last he had heard from her.

That was years ago.

The question 'what if?' had gone round in is mind for years, but on account of how he had never heard anything or any more from her, he eventually forgot about it. Especially when his bonafide bredrins told him about phantom pregnancies, and assured him that having a child that you never see is like having no child at all. Those words were very reassuring.

He had since forgotten about Verna.

"You may have forgotten about her," Amos told him, "but she hasn't forgotten about you. Not since you strike it rich anyway. It looks to me, Johnny, like your chickens have come home to roost."

Johnny wanted to explain things to the detective, but he didn't even know who this guy was.

"Did I not introduce myself?" Amos said, turning to his passenger and handing him a business card. New ones that he had got printed with the legend: *Baby father bounty hunter — we find 'em and bring 'em in.*

"Yeah, I can understand where you're coming from," Amos said, reading Johnny's thoughts, "and I can even sympathise, because I've been there and done all that and been cleaned out by 'nuff baby mothers myself. Trust me 'pon dat. But right now things don't work out like that no more. You see, if you have a pickney with a woman, then you have to understand that it's a fifty-fifty business. That means whatever you have, fifty percent of it belongs to she, you get me? That's what most judges in court would say nowadays. She's got every right to take you and skin you. After all, a pickney is not just for Christmas. Or you nuh know dat?"

Johnny glared at Amos, as if to say, 'Of course I know that, what do you take me for?'

"I hope you're going to come quietly, and not lead me down the road of the well-trodden 'ruff stuff'," Amos said as he slowed his Vitara down at the traffic lights leading into the Blackwall Tunnel.

Johnny saw his chance and took it. He shoved Amos

aside and made a dash for freedom. Jumping out of the passenger side, he legged it across the dual carriageway, dicing with death. Amos had been through all this before. He knew baby fathers better than they knew themselves. He had given Johnny a rope to hang himself, and Johnny had gripped it tight with both hands. He wouldn't have thought very much of Johnny if he hadn't made at least one attempt to escape. In fact, he himself had made similar attempts to escape when he was also a baby father on the run, and it had ended up bad for him too.

Amos used to be a rugby player. He was quick on his feet, and the old flying tackle still played an important part in his repertoire. He also put his life at risk as he chased his quarry across the motorway and up on the verge onto the pavement above. Just before Johnny made it to safety, Amos brought him crashing to the ground, flat on his face.

Johnny was spluttering. Couldn't believe what had happened. He was out of breath. He who had thought that all this sex was keeping him fit, was suddenly realising he wasn't all that after all. Or at least he wasn't as fit as this big guy who looked out of condition but was able to bring him down with just one tackle.

Still, he wasn't going to go down without a fight. He brought his fist up and threw it at Amos's face.

That was a mistake . . .

If there was one thing that really got up Amos's goat, it was getting hit when he was going about trying to execute his legitimate business. What was it with all these serial baby fathers that they were so quick to throw a punch at any Tom, Dick or Harry as the case may be? What was with them? If they weren't trying to beat up on their women they were trying to beat up on any man who stood in their way. A man like Amos who was just trying to make them see sense and come to terms with the devastation they had created in life and to live with it, was an easy target.

Amos wished that once, just once, he would buck up on a baby father who had seen the light and said 'Fair cop, you've got me, it's about time I took responsibility for the mess I've made of my life and other people's lives.' But that was never the case. He wished all these men would appreciate the pleasures of taking care of their own child, of watching that child as it grows every day with a smile on its face. He recalled how he had felt with the birth of his first beautiful daughter. He didn't want to acknowledge it at first, but then he saw her and knew immediately that she was his. Surprisingly, there was no flesh of my flesh, blood of my blood feeling. At least not immediately. But from the shape of the baby's head and the sizable chops that matched his own, there was no doubt that this was the flesh of his flesh. Even though she was several complexions lighter than him (he would have to check back in his family history for that one) not to talk of her red hair, the child seemed to know immediately that he was her father, and looked up to him lovingly with a smile and an appreciation of who he was, looking to him for protection. When you go through that with a child, it is difficult to understand how men still go about their business not really bothered whether they have a child out there or not. As far as Amos could see, such men were callous and, if it was up to him to hold forth and fight with the rod of correction and to chop these runaway baby fathers with it, then so be it. When he thought about it, he was doing society at large a big favour.

Like an injured lion — hurting but not down, Amos became angrier and resorted to some moves that he had learned in martial arts lessons long before he became a baby father bounty hunter. Moves which had come in handy several times already, and would no doubt prove useful many more times.

Johnny didn't know what hit him. He was being slapped about like the baddie in a cheap Hong Kong flick. The only thing that he could do was cry "Help!"

Luckily for Johnny, help came in the form of a stray dog, who seemed to have taken a liking to Amos's bum. The detective let out a loud yelp as the canine's fangs sank into his bottom. This wasn't the first time he had been bitten in the behind by an unrestrained hound, but it was the most painful, because the dog's jaws seemed to be clenched like a vice to his buttocks.

Johnny didn't stop to thank the Lord, but took the opportunity to sprint down the road as quickly as he could, until he was way out of sight and safe.

As he ran, Johnny thought back to Verna. He now recalled that he had been doubly protected. When a woman told you she was on the pill, you generally took her word for it, like a green light saying, 'Come on down, don't even stop to think about it, just fill up that tank.' Yet he had used two condoms on top of that, just to make sure. That's why he subsequently lost all faith in any kind of contraception, and he ended up having kids all over the place. Because if the pill and a condom couldn't keep his seed in check, then nothing could. Yes, he totally blamed that session with Verna for his baby fathering predicament. If she hadn't told him that she was pregnant, despite taking every precaution, he might never have got himself into all this mess in the first place.

He was adamant that he wasn't going to share his wealth with a woman that he didn't even know. He would sooner burn up his remaining millions. He didn't mind splashing out a little on the youth, if it could be proved in a court of law that he was the father, but he wasn't going to let Verna near a penny of that money. Why should he? If the youth was his, why had she deprived him of any contact all these years?

She had another thing coming if she thought she could just rope in and take a slice of his dunza.

4/WAKE ME UP BEFORE YOU GO-GO

a) 'The Hairy Palm Sunday'
Hold the shaft in one hand, with the head sticking up. Using the well-oiled palm of your other hand, slowly and sensitively massage the head. Reverse directions every once in a while.

b) 'Push Here To Start'
Gently insert one finger deeply into her vagina and, when she's ready, insert a second. Then take your thumb and place it against her anus. Don't insert it. Instead, press there while you move your fingers.

Gussie looked forward to seeing Carmel again the way a child looks forward to Christmas morning. He was well aware that a pretty face did not equate to love. He had been down that road and didn't want to go there again. Each time he had made the mistake of confusing love with beauty he had ended up paying for it dearly. He now accepted that beauty is only skin deep, something everybody had been trying to get across to him for years, and that it is easier for a camel to pass through the eye of a needle than for a man looking for beauty to find true love.

With Carmel, though, it was different. He loved her for more reasons than brains. Gussie couldn't believe that he had already started thinking of a future with her. Here at last was the kind of woman he wanted to spend some serious quality time with. With her wealth and his business sense, they could be the Becks and Posh Spice of the black community.

She still hadn't called him. He had expected that she would at least thank him for the champagne. Maybe she was so used to getting gifts from men that she didn't feel that she needed to thank anybody. That was the way with some of these rich girls, they were spoiled rotten. But that wasn't going to put him off. He tried to think of the most reasonable thing to do. He decided to play it by ear.

He thought about it. She had made the first move. He had made the second move. Now it was her turn.

Finally, by eleven o'clock at night, he couldn't take it any more. He called her.

The phone was answered after only two rings. Gussie recognised the voice at the other end.

"Hi, is Carmel around?"

"Who wants to know?"

"It's Gussie."

"Gussie?! No, she isn't."

"Did she get the champagne?"

"Yes."

"Well, do you know when she'll be back?"

"No."

Gussie sighed. "By the way . . . I didn't quite catch your name."

"I didn't give it," Ben replied.

"Look, man, no need to stress. I'm just a friend, calling to wish her a happy birthday."

"Well, you did that already."

"Okay, tell her I called anyway."

He didn't know if Ben quite heard it because he heard the click of disconnection just before he uttered the last word.

To say that Gussie had lost his composure would be to under-represent his true feelings. He paced up and down his room, his heart racing, his breath coming in short bursts, his fists clenching and unclenching. The bwoy deserved a box. If the geezer thought he was going to give up that easy, he had another thing coming. As far as Gussie was concerned, this wasn't just about Carmel anymore, this was personal.

Likewise, who was Gussie kidding if he thought that he was easily going to succeed in getting Ben to throw in the towel.

He phoned again the next morning. Still Ben answered. And later again that afternoon. Still Ben answered. Then later again that evening. By this time, Ben had had enough.

"No she's not in. Can't you get the message? Piss off. Stop being a nuisance."

Gussie really, really REALLY wanted this girl, and if all that stood between him and her was a big beefcake idiot like her boyfriend, he was willing to take up the challenge.

* * *

If thoughts could kill, Linvall would be a dead man right now. Marcia didn't care what his excuse was going to be, if he was wotless enough to forget about the most important school visit of their son's life, he might as well be dead.

She looked at her watch again and sighed helplessly. Still no sign of him. Well, she had given him his last chance.

For once, the minicab company didn't waste her time. With precise efficiency, the cab was outside her home just minutes after she called. She climbed into the front passenger seat. It was the first time she had seen a Suzuki Vitara jeep being used as a minicab. That didn't bother her, as long as it got to Brixton High on time. The last thing she needed was to show up late when she intended to beg for her wayward son's right to attend school.

Everybody had warned Marcia to keep away from Linvall when they first met — her family and friends and even some of *his* family and friends. Her parents were dismayed that their daughter would take up with someone they considered a ragamuffin. "And he is a raggamuffin," her father had insisted, "just look at his table manners, look at those clothes, the way he talks . . . I'm sure he takes drugs!"

Jamaican fathers will be Jamaican fathers, and Marcia's dad had not slaved for thirty years in this country, eventually setting up a successful Jamaican fast food restaurant and managing to send his daughter to a good school, only to see her throw it away on a "no good loafer." What baffled him the most about his daughter's choice of boyfriend, was that he wasn't even handsome. "Yuh see how de bwoy ugly so?" he would ask his wife every night as they lay in bed. Why was Marcia with him? His daughter was attractive. In her teenage days she always had a string of handsome boys running after her. She had matured and become an even more attractive woman. Sure she was his daughter, but she had the same melting eyes as her mother and the same sparkling smile that had made him fall in love with the missus many years before. So why did she waste her time with this Linvall?

Marcia had often wondered the same thing. But like as always, rationale and reasoning go out the window when you are in love. Okay, he hadn't been to university, but qualifications weren't everything and she was sure that it wouldn't be long before her father was commending Linvall's photographic skills. Whatever faults he had back then, she wasn't interested in checking other men as her girlfriends were always suggesting. She was happy that Linvall was her man, all he had to do was prove that he cared about his woman and his child and everything would be sweet.

How could she explain to her friends and family? Linvall used to make her feel so fine when she was alone with him, in bed, far away from the hustle and bustle of street life. He could make her cold nights hot, get her humming. Back in those days, she remembered with fondness, she loved him so much she would often stay awake kissing his deep brown skin from belly button to ear lobe, listening to his strong heart beating, playing with every hair on his chest as he lay asleep.

"Excuse me madam, you look lost in your thoughts, like you could do with some help. Allow me to offer my services . . ."

Marcia looked up for the first time since climbing in the cab. She studied the handsome, smiling features of the elegantly dressed driver, the owner of the deep voice. He didn't look like a minicab driver at all.

"Amos Butler," he said in his slightly gruff accent. "Most of my friends call me Amo."

A smooth and stylish, deep-bronze coloured man in his late forties who used Magic Shave rather than a razor, his hair relaxed and slicked back with Dax hair oil into a short, wet-look style, his fingernails manicured, his dark suit immaculate, the rings on his fingers expensive, and a shine on his face. Since cleaning up his act, Amos gave the impression of being a dashing dandy from the pages of Ebony, if slightly chubbier.

"Listen, I know it's probably none of my business, but is everything alright? You look like you just dropped out of the sky."

"Everything is not alright," Marcia admitted looking at her watch again. She still had fifteen minutes to get to the school. She would make it, no thanks to her husband. She was still angry and would deal with Linvall later.

"What's up?" Amos asked, "did your ride not show up?"

"You know what men are like — unreliable!" Marcia snapped.

"Hey, please!" Amos raised his hand in protest.

"Don't make judgements about me when you hardly know me. There are many different types of men and I'm of a type that don't know the meaning of 'unreliable'."

Amos assured her that there were men like himself who were sensitive and gave as much care, concern and tenderness as they desired from their women. Marcia refused to believe it, so they were deadlocked for a moment.

Before she knew it, the jeep was pulling up outside Brixton High.

"Are you going to be in there long, or do you want me to wait for you and drop you back home afterwards?"

Marcia eyed the man again, his well-cut mohair suit, the white silk shirt, colourful tie. She had to admit that he intrigued her. It was the manner in which he conducted himself and the way he talked, as well as the way he made her feel at ease talking to him. He was nothing like the cab drivers she had previously met.

"That's very kind of you," she replied, paying her fare as she spoke. "It's all right, I'll be able to make my way home by bus."

"My pleasure . . ." Amos insisted with a broad smile as he jumped out of the driver's side and went quickly round to the other side to open the passenger door open for her. " . . .but I wouldn't dream of it. I insist."

'At least the man's got some manners,' Marcia thought, as she stepped down.

* * *

If only Linvall had arrived five minutes earlier. It had taken him ages to get home, with the fear of his woman's wrath 'tailgating' him all the way.

Okay, he was half an hour late and, yeah, Marcia was always impatient, but she could still be waiting. She had to be . . .

Personally, he didn't see why it was such a big thing for him to be there at the school, but Marcia did. He felt she could just have easily taken a cab and sorted things out with the headmistress herself. What difference would it make if one parent was there or two? It would have been almost as quick and would save him a lot of time that he could ill afford. Time waits for no one. He had his business to be getting on with. He wanted to be rich as much as the hungry man wants bread, as much as the choking man wants air. To become rich he had to seize the time and the opportunities. He had explained to Marcia that he needed to start work early, stay late and work tirelessly in between.

Even as late as he was running, if Linvall had decided against getting his rocks off at the last minute, he could have just made it. But, even pressed for time, he reasoned that it was worth risking everything for a little soldering. You see, as far as he was concerned, it was virtually impossible to be taking photos of naked woman without getting all horny, and before you knew it you and the model were ripping each other's clothes off and leaving a trail of bedraggled expensive clothes on the floor.

He was hardly able to believe his good fortune. He had thought that a woman like porn queen Charmaine Charming wouldn't even consider him. She had been dropped off at the session by her boyfriend, who looked mean to say the least. But he had runnings to take care of and, somewhat reluctantly, had left his honey with this randy-looking photographer.

Damn! Linvall was thinking, it was going to be hard to resist. Charmaine looked so good, he didn't know whether to eat her or say hello.

The session was barely over when Charmaine turned to Linvall and said, "Look, it's getting late, but if you hurry and don't do any fancy stuff we could still get a quick one in before my boyfriend comes back. We'll have to be really quick."

Linvall could hardly believe his ears. He had wanted some illicit sex for so long, and now it seemed that the opportunity was staring him in the face. Charmaine and him?! "Yes!" Linvall half-shouted, punching his fist in the air triumphantly. This was definitely a result. Not just a result, but THE result. She was irresistible, no matter how little time he had. If only he had managed to lose some weight before today, if only he had managed to get to the barber's as he had been trying to get to all week.

His heart pumped away furiously, trying to jump out of his mouth. This was it, this was really it. He was going to get laid. No Marcia here to stop him banging away. He could hardly contain the excitement in his trousers. It was like a dream. Was this all really happening?

"Race you to the finish line," she teased.

He grinned. That was a race that he knew he could win. He dropped his trousers. To his surprise, he hadn't worn any underpants that morning.

Charmaine reached out and grabbed him.

"Is it defective?" she asked.

Linvall looked down at his penis in horror. "No way," he insisted.

"Then why does it curl like a banana?"

He didn't have time to answer, because Charmaine started yanking, as if she was trying to straighten him up. She must have been brought up on a farm, because her hands were made for milking cows.

"Aaaaaaargh!" Linvall cried out, but it didn't seem to do any good. Charmaine just kept on yanking. Somehow, she managed to straighten him up.

"All right, where's your condom?" she said.

"Condom?" Linvall sounded like he didn't know the meaning of the word.

"Yeah, condom, you know rubbers. You don't think I would let you anywhere near me without one, do you?"

Linvall started panicking. He knew there was one somewhere in the studio, but he couldn't remember where. All he knew was that he had hidden a pack so well that Marcia wouldn't find it when she came sniffing. Hidden it too well, apparently

In a panic he went through everything, knocking over chairs, tables, lamps and anything else in his way in the process. The place looked like a hurricane had breezed through.

"Hurry up," she demanded.

"I know they're here somewhere," he said. "Look Charmaine, I'll just pop down the road to the petrol station. Wait there, don't go anywhere. I'll be right back."

Linvall ran as fast as his feet would carry him. Just his luck that when he got to the petrol station there was a big queue of people waiting to be served. As much as he was screwing, he had to wait his turn. None of the others there had ever seen a man so desperate to buy condoms before.

"I hope she's worth it," said the attendant as he handed him over a pack of threes.

As luck would have it, Linvall only had a £20 note in his pocket. The attendant took so much time in sorting out the change that Linvall, in his urgency, shouted "Keep it," and then legged it back to the studio fast.

Unfortunately for him, Charmaine's ruffneck boyfriend was already there waiting to take her home.

As if matters couldn't get any worse for Linvall, when he went to his car later, he discovered that someone had let down the air in all four tyres.

* * *

Amos was still outside Lacquan's school waiting when Marcia emerged from her meeting with the headmistress.

"Your chariot awaits you," he announced with a bow, holding the door of the Vitara open for her.

Marcia had a scowl on her face, but Amos felt that it was not for him.

"By the way, I didn't tell you, I just flew in from New York — first class of course — the only way to fly!" Amos laughed, self-consciously as he drove her home. "I should have flown on Concorde like I usually do, but it doesn't land at Gatwick. Have you ever flown Concorde?"

Marcia sized the man up silently and shook her head. Why was a cab driver flying Concorde she wondered. He had to be lying.

"You haven't? Believe me, that's the only way to fly. Of course it's all first class, so you get treated really well. The flight's so quick, I hardly ever get a chance for a nap because four hours later you're in London. Then when you arrive at the airport, you never get any trouble from Customs and Immigration when you step off Concorde."

Clearly, Marcia was not in the mood for chatting. She had only just managed to save her son from being expelled or excluded or whatever else they wanted to call it. She was still screwing about Linvall not being there. She wasn't prepared to take that crap from him any longer. It wasn't good enough. It was like Linvall refused to grow up. He was in his late twenties with a son to look after, but still behaved as if he was an immature teenager with no responsibilities. She just didn't understand him. He was like an alien species to her. What was it that possessed him to want to behave like he did? Did he not value his son's life, his son's future? Why could she never rely on him where Lacquan was concerned. Why was it she who had to look for work and do a degree to provide them with some security? Why did he treat her like his mother's substitute and why did she have to become the father to Lacquan that he refused to be? She acknowledged that Lacquan needed male influences, otherwise she would show Linvall the door. But Lacquan was in the throes of puberty, very soon he'd start shaving and things like that. They say sons brought up by single mothers develop problems later on, because all the love and caring a husband would have drained from her the mother channels into her son, which might seem overwhelming to him. Marcia wasn't sure. She simply felt that Linvall had to do his job.

Marcia sighed. She came from a very proud family, and a lot of that pride had rubbed off on her. She wanted her son to have some of that pride, too. She didn't want him to be like his father, but the kind of man her parents would have liked her to have met when she was a teenager. A black man with some power in the world. Not a pop singer or a photographer or an athlete, but a lawyer or a doctor or a politician, something like that. Something constructive.

"Guess what I was doing over in the Big Apple?" Amos continued.

Marcia wasn't in the mood for guessing, so he told her anyway.

"I was over there checking some of my people dem. I had a great time. I spent a lot of time watching the chat shows on TV. You know Donny and Marie Osmond have got one. Even old Ainsley Harriot has got one. I got to meet Queen Latifah and went on her chat show — The Latifah Show. It was all about a girl whose father abandoned her as a child and she became hooked on drugs, but then Latifah brought the two of them together and they hugged and cried . . . It was very touching. Afterwards we went to this fabulous Caribbean restaurant called Negril on 363 West 23rd St, New York. There, I got to take pictures of myself with Latifah, but some flipping girl in the background wouldn't come out of my picture! Did you see Latifah singing 'Who The Cap Fit' on that Bob Marley tribute from Jamaica on the 4th of December? Believe me, that was one of the best performances I have seen in my life. I must have watched the video of it two hundred times already."

Amos glanced over to Marcia expecting to see her captivated by his story. To his surprise she wasn't, so he decided to change tact.

"I bet you must have a lot of male admirers," he said interestedly, "an attractive woman like you."

" 'Woman shall not live by male admirers alone'," Marcia laughed. "Anyway, you know what they say, a good man is hard to find. If you know any good men, a really good man, and he's available, give him my number."

Amos straightened himself up. Raised an eyebrow.

"In that case, if I may say so, you've just found yourself another admirer. A really good one. So tell me, what are you up to in the next few days. I have a lot of free time. Maybe we could link up."

It was a statement more than a question. Amos was very confident of himself. 'And why shouldn't he be?', Marcia thought, after all he had a certain charm about him.

'This is one fine gal', Amos thought to himself. 'Even a blind man could look at her and see she is irresistible'.

"So do you have any admirer in particular, a boyfriend? A husband?"

"Why do you ask?"

"Oh I noticed that you weren't wearing a wedding ring," he said glancing down at her finger, and I was wondering whether it was because beautiful women aren't allowed to wear wedding rings. I think I heard that somewhere?"

"Of course not," Marcia said. "But I do have a husband . . . At least I did have before he didn't bother showing up for the most important appointment in his son's life. I'm not too sure if I want him any longer."

"He's the guy who didn't show up to pick you up?"

Marcia kissed her teeth, she didn't need to answer.

"Well, if you don't mind my saying it, I think he must be an idiot. What kind of a man leaves his woman waiting in vain? I didn't believe that those type of men still existed. If you were my woman, I would never disrespect you like that. Look, I know how you must be feeling, but don't mind him. Believe me, there are some nice and decent sensitive men out there, real romantic types who will treat you good. You women nowadays just aren't looking in the right places."

Marcia wasn't convinced.

"So what about you?" she asked. "With all your charm, I bet you've had more than your fair share of women."

Amos put on his best 'down and lonely' voice. The one that women always fell for.

"To tell you the truth, I've made some mistakes. But all of that is in the past. All I want now is one woman to cherish. I'm a one woman kind of guy, but I'm still looking for the perfect woman to call my own."

He stared out of the window for a moment, reflectively, as he waited at a stop sign.

"Well, who's perfect?" Marcia offered, "I don't know one person who's perfect."

"You're pretty close to perfect," he said, turning towards her. He had wanted to compliment her for most of the journey, but couldn't figure out the best way to tell her what was on his mind. There was something about this sweet woman that told him she needed his gentle touch. The signs told him that this might still turn out exactly the way he desired if he played his cards right.

"Don't you think you should find out a bit more about me before you make statements like that?" Marcia asked, clearly impressed.

Amos looked deep into her eyes with as much sincerity as the situation warranted.

"Yes, it would help if I got to know you better, but I like what I see already."

"So what is it exactly that you like? You like my legs?"

"Yes, and your arms and your neck, your eyes, your mouth . . ." he said with a smile.

"But that's just my body. You started off saying I was perfect, now I find out that you don't mean *me* at all, just my body."

Marcia enjoyed this friendly jousting. She didn't need a shoulder to cry on to get Linvall's let-down off her chest, she just needed an ego boost.

Amos's flattery worked. When someone laughs and harmonises with you, you feel you enjoy their company better. It didn't matter that Marcia knew she was no more perfect than anybody else, it was just nice to hear kind words after feeling unloved, unwanted and unappreciated. Amos's compliments had enabled her to hold her head a little higher. She caught him undressing her with his eyes and felt half-naked, but she didn't mind. She felt very relaxed with him.

"What do I have to do to get you to come out to dinner with me?" he asked, as he held the passenger door open for her when they finally got back to her house.

"You would have to offer a candlelit dinner for two and a sip or two of sparkling white wine," she smiled.

Amos beamed broadly, a glint in his eye.

"I can do better, how about a bottle or two of cold champagne?"

Marcia agreed, to Amos's delight. He looked up at the heavens gratefully. He was always thankful for whatever life offered him, but this was a bonus.

In Marcia's case, she knew that men were prone to more than a little bull. However, she was intrigued by this guy and wanted to find out if he was for real.

Amos smiled a big and broad smile and puffed up his chest.

* * *

Carmel couldn't figure out why Ben hadn't flown to the States on her birthday as he said he would. She still couldn't believe he was spending so much time with her. He had barely left her side. What was with this change? She had questioned him about it, and he had said something about how much he had neglected her and that he realised that his job wasn't more important than his relationship. She smelled a rat. She knew him too well. Before the change, all he ever talked about was how much money he was making and how much money he was going to make and how his job came before his relationship in all matters. "That's how I got to where I am today," Ben had always been fond of saying. "So few men are prepared to make sacrifices to reach the top any more. Look at your average black man, how many of them are prepared to make sacrifices, believe you me. Believe you me, there's nothing a black man can do for you, Carmel. Us white guys may not be perfect, but compared to these black guys I see nowadays, we're as near to perfection as you're going to get."

Carmel sniffed. Was Ben trying to tell her something?

"Maybe we should go on that holiday right now?" Ben suggested. "Only maybe we should just go away for a long weekend? How about a romantic 5 star weekend in Venice."

So, now it's only a weekend? Carmel said nothing.

* * *

Caroline knew for certain that something was up. During the past few weeks, she had made love to Beres so many times, she had lost count. No matter how hard she tried, he was always coming up with some excuse or other, but never coming. Either it was so late, he was tired. Or it was too hot or too cold. Or he had a headache. Or he didn't want to wake the baby in the flat next door, so he would decline an orgasm. A few times he said he was too sore, or he had to get up early in the morning, or he simply wasn't in the mood. He had even pretended to be asleep, pretended to be sunburned, claimed he had cramp in his toes, a splinter in his finger, got it caught in his zipper or that he had got into a fight and someone had kicked him in the testicles. He had even had the nerve one time to suggest that it was the wrong time of the month for him to have a climax. His excuses had got so thin recently, that he had taken to coming home drunk and disorderly.

Caroline wasn't mad about it. After all, what good

would that do?

Her girlfriends started urging her to go out with them. At first she said she was too busy, but then one thing led to another and, before she knew it, she was staying out most nights and partying. Then she was unfaithful one time . . .

After that first time, she found it easy to be unfaithful again and again. She figured that Beres suspected as much, because he was saying 'I love you' less frequently.

She was looking forward to him moving out, but Beres didn't seem to be in too much of a hurry himself. She had dropped several hints, but then he would look at her with those woeful eyes of his and, before she knew it, he would be saying that he needed a little more time.

Beres still couldn't believe it. It was the same every time. First he'd be hard and stiff from thinking about sex all day and then when the moment and opportunity came, there he was with the orgasm rushing inside him, but refusing to actually come out. But when he lay on his bed alone and started thinking about his ex-wife, it erupted just like that. Almost as if he was suffering from post-mature ejaculation.

But how was he going to explain that to Caroline? Although his inability to achieve orgasm was of paramount importance to him, he was unwilling to suggest that they invite his ex-wife into the bedroom with them. That idea seemed somewhat extreme and inappropriate.

As much as Beres wanted to come clean, he couldn't. He should have, but he couldn't. He didn't want to hurt Caroline's feelings. He was sure that she was still madly, deeply in love with him and thought it was better that he weaned her off gradually.

* * *

"So, did you get the champagne?"

"What champagne?"

"On your birthday?"

"From you?"

"Yes."

"No. Not from you?"

A bottle of Bollinger."

"That was from you?" She couldn't believe it. Had she misunderstood something? Surely not. Now she felt embarrassed. "I'm sorry, I didn't realise."

"Who did you think it was from?"

She thought about it for a moment, but decided against saying.

"Yes, it was from me. I gave it to . . . what'shisname."

"Ben."

"That's right, the flowerpot man. Are you and him an item or something?"

"Or something."

"Well, I hope you don't mind me saying so, but you can do better than that. A whole heap better than that."

"Hey, that's my fiancé you're talking about."

"Oh, I'm sorry."

"Only kidding."

"I don't understand you."

"That's hardly surprising, nobody does."

"Really, you come across to me as being an intelligent woman. That guy's just not you. If you ask me."

* * *

"Yaow, Linvall!"

He turned to see someone calling him from a criss-looking red Merc. He screwed his eyes. It was Mario Molinari.

Linvall sighed. He knew what was coming. Mario was a bragging big head, but he was also one of the most successful paparazzi's out there. Always bragging about one thing or another, usually about how many women he had pulled. But Mario had recently lost his balls. It wasn't a joke, he had actually got his balls shot off by the jealous husband of a woman he had shagged and now walked with a severe limp, and had subsequently developed a bitter hatred of all Bajan men. Despite this, Mario still went around with some of the crissest women, even though everybody knew he couldn't actually do anything with them.

"I've just come back from my accountants," Mario bragged, "look how much money I made last year." Linvall glanced at the final total. £800,000!

"Syndication rights, me old mate," Mario continued. "That's where the money is nowadays. Syndication and a lot of hard graft. You just can't make any real money while your mind is on women all the time."

It's amazing what your old accounts book can tell you about the life you used to live and make you face up to who you have become. Later at home, Linvall sat down going through his old accounts book. It seemed so long ago that he was earning seventy grand. Yes, that's what it said in his accounts book, and this was back when seventy grand really was seventy grand. He had earned that in one year — one of his best years. He had become rich and famous by taking pictures of the rich and famous. Back in those days he had taken photographs of nearly every member of the royal family, and had been sworn at by most of them. He was able to charge a lot of money for his pics because there were probably only another twenty guys in the world who were prepared to do what he was prepared to do to get a photograph. Not many other photographers would have hired a helicopter to go chasing royalty. Very few would have agreed to be suspended out of the helicopter by their legs to get the photo. He remembered one time, at a Swiss castle where Princess Diana was holed up. He and a lot of other photographers were camped outside, waiting. Of all the photographers, only Linvall was smart enough to have hired a Mercedes in the same charcoal colour as the princess' escort. When her fleet of Mercs came racing out of the castle at a hundred miles per hour to avoid the paparazzi, Linvall simply jumped in his car and joined the line. As they raced down the mountainside, his adrenaline was rushing and he started to get a buzz.

In front of him were three Benzes — the first one carrying police officers, the second contained the Princess, the third full of bodyguards. Linvall quickly overtook the bodyguards' car. The next time the Princess, sitting on the back seat, turned around, she faced Linvall's camera as he snapped away with one hand while the other held the steering wheel. The horror in her face was evident as she realised what had happened and, through his viewfinder, Linvall saw her desperately urging her chauffeur to relay the news ahead. At the bottom of the mountain was a police roadblock which had obviously been told to let through the first three vehicles. By the time the princess' chauffeur managed to relay the new situation to the people at the checkpoint, Linvall was already through and the police stopped the Mercedes carrying the bodyguards. It took the cops several more kilometres to catch up with Linvall. By then he had got all the pictures he needed.

No wonder he had earned seventy grand in that year, with bottle like that he was worth every penny.

From paparazzi, he had turned to fashion, and seemed to be doing really well. He would have done even better if he hadn't been trying to get the models into the sack as well as on the front covers of *Vogue* and *Cosmo*.

Now, though, the good times were over, and he didn't know if they would ever come back again. In the last few weeks he had called up all his contacts on the press and tried to get freelance work. He needed it, needed the cash, and needed to make a name for himself again. In the old days, the very fact that Linvall was a trendy black photographer with dreadlocks would get him work. Not any more, though. Alas, many of his old contacts had moved on. The new faces that sat in their positions didn't know of Linvall's glory days chasing Princess Di and, quite frankly, didn't care either. There was a new breed of photographer out there — younger, leaner, hungrier and less inclined to waste their talents as an opportunity to bed women.

* * *

Linvall had taken their relationship for granted one too many times.

Marcia had agreed to go to dinner with Amos, not just out of anger with Linvall but because the older man was fun and was there to give her some time, consideration and a hug when she was feeling unappreciated. Nothing more than that.

Amos had insisted on her suggesting a really nice place to eat. As it was a warm day, they had settled for a popular floating restaurant moored on the Thames at the Embankment. Throughout the meal, the detective had been loud and very full of himself, but he was always charming and, yes, she couldn't deny it, she found him attractive and easy to talk to.

'Well,' she thought to herself, 'it's not unusual to sometimes feel you deserve better.'

It was that simple, Marcia reflected. The best, the

very best, was the absolute minimum requirement for any relationship. Not just a best friend or best lover, but the best treatment, the best vibes. She shouldn't have to settle for anything less.

Amos Butler had a taste for the finest things in life. Good wine, a good cigar, good food and good women were things he didn't take lightly. Especially good food. When it came to good food, money was no problem, and he was more than pleased to spend a good portion on this woman he liked so much because of her *je ne sais quoi.* They had talked for hours about all kinds of things and the closer he got to her, the more she was making him smile and, though he held back because her body language was telling him not to rush things, that it was still too early in their relationship, his body, mind and soul were all burning with a deep desire for her. He couldn't understand why she had put up with Linvall's behaviour for so long and, to be honest, looking at it in the cold light of day, neither could she.

Though she was still married, Marcia couldn't help thinking that if she was going to have a scene with anyone it could easily be Amos. The way she felt now after three glasses of champagne, she wouldn't even mind sleeping with the guy.

Of course she wouldn't sleep with him. No sex on a first, second or third date, that was the way she had always been. She didn't want any man thinking she was easy. She sipped at the champagne some more. Maybe this guy only had one thing on his mind, but at least he was making an effort. It was fun going out with Amos as a friend and that was the way it was staying, unless things got worse with Linvall.

"I don't see anything wrong with a little bump and grind," Amos said with a smile. He knew how Marcia would react, because he had tested his opinion on many women before. They always sounded horrified at first. It always took a lot more teasing and coaxing before they would admit that they too saw nothing wrong with it.

"There's more to sex than just bumping and grinding," Marcia said, taking another sip of champagne. "Man shall not live by bump and grind alone. That's why men can never understand women, we're more complex. Feelings complicate things. I spent so many nights awake trying to explain that to Linvall, but he just didn't get it. In most relationships, when something somewhere is wrong, it is usually the man. Believe."

Amos smiled. "Love is like a candy on the shelf. If you want a taste, you have to help yourself. But, you're right, to touch a woman's soul, you've got to have feelings."

"That's nonsense. Total nonsense . . ." Marcia said, throwing her head back in laughter. "Why can't men say what they mean and mean what they say?"

'Yes,' Amos thought to himself, 'I shall have this woman. Linvall is going to lose her. His own fault. Linvall's loss is going to be my gain. I'll show him how to treat a woman right.'

They had finished their meals.

"You're sure I can't change your mind about that bump 'n' grind?"

Marcia declined without hesitation.

"Why do you want to sleep with me?"

"Because you can make me happy, and I can make you happy. I know what you're going through, your husband's . . ."

"You don't know what I'm going through," Marcia laughed. "How could you, you hardly know me."

"But you're a woman, your man done you wrong. Believe me, I know what a woman needs in this situation, some good, good loving."

"But all women are not the same."

"A woman, is a woman, is a woman," Amos insisted with a smile.

If it wasn't for the champagne, Marcia may have thought that Amos was treading on dangerous ground but the bubbly was fizzing around in her head.

"For the time being anyway," she said, "I am married and faithful . . ."

"But I thought you said . . .?"

"That's between me and Linvall."

Marcia sighed. Since he failed to show up to discuss his son's educational future, Linvall was only half the man he used to be in her eyes. She had put his loving to the test and he had failed miserably.

"You fight your natural feelings though, don't you?" Amos said. "I've noticed that about you. It's like suppressing your passions, and a woman should never suppress her passions."

"I don't suppress my passions."

"So what are you going to do about your situation? You've got a man who treats you like he doesn't care about you and you've got a man like me, who wants to take you higher, further than any jumbo jet can take you. How can I prove what I feel about you?"

Marcia sighed again. She advised Amos to be patient and take his time. If he really wanted to prove anything to her he might yet get his chance. If she made things too easy for him he wouldn't appreciate it.

Amos shrugged his shoulders. Marcia was putting up a whole lot of resistance, but he could sense that they were going to work things out eventually.

"So what now?" Amos asked as they stood on dry land afterwards. "Shall we go back to my place for some more champagne?"

"You never give up . . ."

Marcia had had a great time, but she didn't want things to become awkward between them. She didn't want to do anything silly and end up regretting

"You shouldn't be going home to an empty bed," Amos started again, "just come back for one drink. That doesn't mean I'm asking you to stay overnight. But you can if you want . . ."

"We'll see, shall we?" she said, taking his arm but giving nothing away. "I'll come to your place for a drink . . . just one drink. Let's just have one nice drink together and leave it at that. Okay?"

"Your wish is my command," said Amos, executing a mock bow and beaming all over his face. He stuck two fingers in his mouth and whistled for a taxi.

"Peckham Rye!" he told the driver, then held the door open for Marcia in true gentleman style.

* * *

Johnny recognised the numberplates straight away — CRRI55. He didn't waste a second. This time he was hoping to stop all the chasing around, and find out who this criss gal was, and to see if there was anything in it for him — so to speak.

He parked around the corner from the hotel in Mayfair and jumped out of his Porsche. Within moments he was standing in the hotel foyer, his mind ticking all the time. His eyes scanned the surroundings quickly and settled on the young, black hotel porter.

"Yes star, respect!" Johnny walked up to him. "I need some information."

The porter eyed him suspiciously.

"I'm looking for a woman . . ."

"Aren't we all . . ." the porter said in a south London brogue. "What woman exactly?"

"Good looking black gal. Drives the flash Porsche outside. The one with the 'CRRISS' numberplate."

"I can't jus' give you that kinda information, this is a hotel, y'know."

Linvall had already dipped into his pocket and pulled out a £50 note from the wad. He tucked it into the porter's red waistcoat jacket.

"Hold some change."

The porter pulled the note out and examined it briefly. With a neat fold he tucked it into his trouser pocket.

"What information exactly d'you want, sir?" he asked.

"What's her name?"

"Miss Criss."

"Miss Criss? That can't be right."

"That's the only name she goes by."

"And she's staying at this hotel?"

"Yeah."

"What room's she in?"

"I'm afraid that's more than my job's worth."

Johnny slipped him another fifty.

"Room 777 . . . but she's out."

"Did she go out by herself?"

"No, she was with this black guy. Nice, you know, elegant, tall . . ."

"You know where they went?" Johnny asked urgently.

The youth looked about him.

"Hang about," he said and stepped out of the hotel's glass doors to converse with the top-hatted doorman. After a moment, the porter returned.

"He wants some change as well," he said.

Johnny shrugged and pulled another £50 note from his tightly wrapped roll of banknotes and handed it over.

"He says they got into a taxi about an hour ago, to take them to the Savoy."

Johnny thought for a minute. Then he peeled off another £50 note from his wad and tucked it into the porter's waistcoat.

"I don't care how you do it, but as soon as she comes in, call me. There's another hundred in it for you when I get the call. Here's my mobile number. "

Johnny scribbled the number down quickly.

"So this woman, you fancy her or something?" the porter asked.

"Who wants to know?"

"It's just because they seemed to be a bit intimate, you know, her and that bloke."

Johnny didn't need to hear any more. He made his way quickly out of the hotel foyer, knowing that he might be on a wild goose chase. Outside, he gunned the engine of his Porsche and drove away in a screech of tyres.

Several things were going through his mind as he raced down Park Lane, dodging in and out of the evening traffic.

* * *

Linvall had long forgotten that there were more than enough men out there to find his woman attractive. It wasn't that he couldn't see that she was as pretty as a summer's day, and still had that sparkle in her eye that had first attracted him to her all those years ago. When it came to wit, she was as sharp as a razor and could keep a man entertained for hours, when she wasn't being bad-minded and carrying on with some outta order man-hating business. All in all, though, she was a good catch for a better man.

If Linvall was a better man, he wouldn't be trying to get off with different women all the time

It didn't bother Marcia that Amos was a few years older. No, at least he was still relatively fit, which was more than she could say of Linvall who had his head so far up his backside that he didn't have time to go to the gym often enough and keep in trim as he had done in his younger years when he would have thought nothing of going five or six times a week, just so as he could come out looking fine.

No, sadly, Linvall had lost that side of himself and didn't even realise it. Amos, on the other hand, was already losing some of his hair (even though he denied it, she could see that hairline receding at an alarming rate), but that didn't bother her. Right now, she preferred a man who was mature.

It was another few days before Amos saw her again. He invited himself around and overstayed his welcome. He cuddled up behind her and put an arm around her waist. It was all that he could do to stop himself from pouncing on her. He could feel it, it was right there at his fingertips if he wanted it. She didn't even seem to offer up any resistance whatsoever.

They had so much to talk about. As they chatted, he snaked his hand further around her waist, and let it wander upward towards her breast. He felt her stiffen slightly, then relax. With her back to him, he fondled her breasts, toyed with her nipples. Then he licked his finger and let it dive down low between her legs, caressing gently. She moaned slightly. He caressed her buttocks, squeezing playfully, cheekily.

"If you're going to regret this in the morning, we can sleep until the afternoon," he grinned.

"Just go on," she breathed.

Then, before she knew it, his head was below the duvet, and he was biting her bum. She gasped with delight. Somehow, by contorting his body, he found a route from her buttocks to her vagina, and went to work.

Oh my God! She couldn't believe it. Here was another master of the tongue. To have found one black man in a lifetime who knew what to do with it was pure chance, but to have found two in succession was truly a blessing. If anything, Amos had a slight edge over Linvall, if for no reason than he seemed to have an incredible sensitivity in his touch.

He must have been down there for hours, before he eventually rolled her over on her back and, looking deep in each other's eyes, she felt him pushing into her. Deep, deep, *oh my god,* when was it going to stop?

This was the longest, the leanest, the meanest . . .

A thought suddenly occurred to her and she reached down below to make sure that that was what he was inserting in her. She took hold of it by the scruff of the neck and, lo and behold, Amos's manhood snapped its head back and growled at her. It was one of the biggest examples she had ever seen this side of mankind. And, unlike Linvall, he knew what to do with it.

It seemed like he was barely moving . . . He was just looking her straight in the eyes, but she could feel the in and out pumping movement as his piece did its job inside her. Her mind was a thousand confused sensations playing tricks on her, like her vagina was about to explode beneath her. It was incredible.

That was just the first time. Amos barely waited for her to catch her breath again before he had rolled on his back and lifted her on top of him. No, she didn't have to move, he was going to do all the work.

Again, it seemed like he possessed a clockwork cock-a-doodle-doo, because he barely moved yet she could feel it thrusting itself upwards like a piston inside her.

Amos enjoyed himself, too. It wasn't that she was an expert in bed or anything, it was more that she had a beautiful body and a sweet tone of voice. When she started moaning and groaning it was the sweetest sound he had ever heard. Just to hear her turned him on. The more she moaned, the more it drove him wild.

It went on like that for hours. Afterwards they lay still, both taking it in. Both thinking about how pleasurable it had been, but also wondering where this new course would take them.

"So, what now?" she asked.

"I could ask you the same question."

"It was nice."

"Yes, really nice."

"You said that you're not seeing anyone . . ."

He had still not fully made up his mind about her,

whether this was going to be the one. THE woman. She possibly could be. In which case he had to take things cool. Then again, she might not be, in which case he didn't want to lay his cards down immediately. He opted to tell her the truth.

"Well, there is this one lady. Not exactly a girlfriend, no you couldn't call her that . . ."

"What could you call her then?"

"Well, I suppose she's someone I see every now and then."

"A girlfriend, in other words."

"I guess you could say that, but I don't call her that. I'm not betrothed to her or anything."

Well, if he was going to play it cool, she was too.

"So we're consenting adulterers."

"Something like that."

"Well, that's fine."

"Is it? Is it really?"

"Sure, why not?"

"But what do you want?"

"Pretty much the same as you want, I should imagine. Great sex. And some good times together when we're not having sex even."

That wasn't what she wanted at all, and he could sense that. But he was not prepared to commit himself, not after this one sexual adventure. Now that he had satisfied himself, he could play it like he wanted. Marcia was, after all, a married woman.

"So, who is this woman?" she asked.

"Oh, you know, just a woman . . ."

"Does she have a name?"

"Yeah, Pinky."

"Pinky?"

"Penelope . . . everybody calls her Pinky, since she was a kid."

"White or black?"

"Look, let's change the subject. I don't feel too comfortable about talking about her when she's not here."

He left her wondering.

Marcia wondered about a lot of things. It was good sex, but she began to regret herself. She got caught in it before she realised. Linvall had made her so frustrated that she threw caution to the wind.

"Can I see you again?"

"Sure, if you've got the time."

"And the inclination."

She turned and gave him a friendly pat on the cheek.

"Oh, I'm sure I'll have the inclination. You made sure of that, didn't you."

Amos smiled. Women were always commending him for his prowess at sex.

* * *

Men commit adultery every day of their lives anyway. Maybe only with their eyes, but certainly they continually undress passers-by and fantasise about what it would be like to sleep with them. The male sex drive is too strong to expect otherwise.

Take Linvall. He's in a marriage with a woman who has never told him once that she loved him, and who he doesn't see eye to eye with — they are like chalk and cheese. Always bickering. Always disagreeing. In fact, she has a permanent scowl on her face when it comes to any questions of trust and faith. He was well and truly under heavy manners. If he was at a restaurant eating with some woman, he'd have to keep one eye on the clock to make sure that, like Cinderella, he made it home before the clock struck midnight. Even when he went out to parties with his spars, he couldn't have a slow dance with a woman without one of Marcia's 'sistas-in-spirit' coming up to him and telling him that it was time he got his 'skinny' behind home — "There's a good boy . . ."

Even his family, particularly his father, had openly stated that Marcia should come to them if she ever has trouble handling him. And that's exactly what she ends up doing. When problems arise in the relationship, she immediately gets on the phone to Mr. Henry for some insight as to why his son behaves in such and such a way, rather than going to Linvall himself, the alleged source of the problem. It is only after those other measures are exhausted that she approaches him, merely relaying what his highly knowledgeable family have told her.

He had asked her several times not to involve his family in their personal affair. He had tried to point out that, although his relatives mean well, they simply don't have a clue as to what they're talking about. As far as he was concerned, their proclaimed objectivity was ultimately covered by a blanket of bias that, because they are family, cannot help but distort what may or may not be troubling the relationship.

"My only concern is fostering a strong and meaningful relationship," he had said to Marcia. "Yet this can never happen when intrusive noses are constantly butting in. A relationship is about two people coming together and being one, not three or four or five. That's all I want, that's all I've ever wanted. To simply love you without an audience."

Linvall was thinking about all these things as he potted away absent-mindedly at the back of their Brixton home. Marcia had been on his case all week about sorting out the mess in the garden, and even though he was dog-tired from having been at the studio all night long developing film and printing pics, he was nevertheless getting it done.

He was just about to pull the lawn mower out of the shed when a voice from over the next fence said, "Linvall, glad I caught you, been meaning to have a word in your ear."

Linvall poked his head up to see his neighbour, old Mr. Finn, giving him the old nod and a wink.

"Blimey," Mr. Finn continued, "the noises that were coming from your house last night were incredible. Don't you think that kind of lovemaking is too loud for this neighbourhood?"

Linvall looked at him nonplussed.

The neighbour pointed up to the bedroom that

overlooked the garden.

"Maybe it would help if you remembered to close the windows next time, eh?"

Johnny looked up. Indeed the bedroom window was wide open. But the neighbour must be mistaken.

"Don't you mean two nights ago?" he offered.

"No, two nights ago was you, I can tell your moaning anywhere. Two nights ago was loud, but not as loud as last night," the neighbour insisted. "Last night was more of a howling than a moaning."

Linvall dropped the rake that he had been poodling about with and rushed inside. His woman was as yet out, but he rushed up to the bedroom and pulled back the duvet. He studied the bedsheet microscopically. He lifted it up to his nose.

Indeed, if he wasn't mistaken, there was a quaint whiff of S-E-X. That in itself was no proof. It could have lingered from their great night of passion a couple of nights ago, when he had given what he believed was his best performance ever, while Marcia was sitting twiddling her thumbs with an unsatisfied look on her face and saying, "You seem really exhausted, what have you been doing to yourself, I expect my man to keep himself in shape, you know, you're not just here to be a pretty face, you're supposed to do your duties also . . ."

With a closer inspection of the bedsheet he found a hair. Not just any hair, but a curly grey hair. The discovery sent him reeling. He didn't have any grey hair, and neither did Marcia. He held the hair up to the light to make sure that he wasn't dreaming. He wasn't.

5/THE NITTY GRITTY

a)'The Double Whammy'
Bring both hands down on the shaft. Some are so big they require both hands. If you partner's doesn't, then use the other hand to caress and lightly flutter his balls. If both hands fit along the length of the shaft then move them together, up and down in a pumping motion.

b) 'From the Outside'
Lay your free hand over the lower part of your partner's abdomen. Experiment by applying different kinds of pressure with the top hand while fingers from your other hand are inside her vagina.

From the viewpoint of the male child, perhaps the worst tragedy that could befall him is to be denied the opportunity to know his father. In an age where the single parent mother has come to be accepted as a norm, too little attention has been paid to the psychological scars this exclusive relationship can leave.

The door swung open and Marcia — illuminated only by the light from the hallway — tumbled into the living room, followed by Amos, who was attempting to bite her ear while she fought him off half-heartedly, laughing playfully all the time.

Linvall's nostrils flared up.

"What's going on?" he asked sternly.

Marcia and Amos stopped, dead in their tracks. She

flicked on the light switch and remained staring at her husband sitting in the armchair with anger in his eyes. She sighed a sigh of frustration, then kissed her teeth.

"What's going on?" Linvall repeated.

Amos gave Marcia a 'Do you know this bum?' look.

She sighed again.

"What the hell are you doing here?" Marcia asked.

Linvall couldn't believe his ears.

"Yeah what the hell *are* you doing here?" Amos repeated after her.

"*You!*" Linvall had only just recognised the detective. "What the hell are you talking about?!"

Linvall's response served for both Marcia and Amos's questions.

Marcia turned to Amos, then to Linvall, then back to Amos. His eyes flicked from Linvall to Marcia then back to Linvall. Linvall simply waited. It was a stand-off.

"You better go," Marcia urged Amos.

The detective gave her a quizzical look as if to say 'Are you sure you want me to leave you alone with this lunatic'?

Marcia insisted. Amos mumbled incoherently before turning reluctantly towards the door.

"Call me later," he told her.

Amos withdrew somewhat reluctantly.

Linvall waited until he had heard the outside door slam shut.

"What are you doing with him?" Linvall asked. "I can't believe . . . You know who he is . . .?"

"Yes, I know who he is. He's a great guy," Marcia

said triumphantly.

"That's what you think," Linvall snapped. "It will end in tears, you'll see. Don't tell me you're actually checking him."

"I never said that."

"You don't need to say it, I can see it in your eyes. You've slept with him, haven't you?"

"So what if I have? Linvall, you may think you're clever, but don't come acting the wronged husband with me. Any infidelity that I may have been engaged in, is nothing to compared to the amount of times you contemplate being unfaithful every day."

"What?" Linvall was confused. "How many times . . ."

"Yes, for your information, Amos has been watching you very closely this past week. On my behalf, he mounted a surveillance operation. He's giving me the file and, I must say, I can't believe that you make that many passes at women every day."

Linvall still did not register. "Come again?"

"Firstly, why you never tell me that you were taking pornographic photos?"

"P-p-p-p-p . . ." Linvall could not bring himself to repeat the word.

"Secondly, why can't you take photos without trying to get in bed with the models?"

"Me?" Linvall cried, cowering slightly because he expected a slap to come flying through the air and striking him at any moment. But no slap came. It was as if Marcia was not bothered.

"There's no need to deny it. I've got it all on tape. You know how bugs work? They pick up every sound you make in that studio. If you fart, it picks it up."

Linvall could have collapsed. That detective! How low could a brotha go?

"You see, Linvall, you're the last person to say anything about me checking anyone. I've had enough of you. Enough of having to keep an eye on you twenty-four seven to make sure that you don't get off with anyone. Why should I have to make sure you keep your tun-tun in check? Eeenh?"

Linvall was so ashamed that he didn't know where to hide his face.

"And another thing, Linvall, I've decided it's your turn to look after your son. Yes, I've already tried everything I know. For years I was bringing Lacquan up alone, remember? He needs the father's touch now."

"Why do you always have to bring that up? I know I wasn't around all those years. But we've been through it enough."

"Because all you've given me these last thirteen years is sex and stress. You must think I'm a fool bringing up your kid. I gave birth to our son. When I looked into his tiny, perfect face, your eyes stared back at me. He was supposed to be a miracle — the embodiment of our love. I couldn't wait for you to see him. I waited and waited and waited in that maternity ward by myself. In the end, you came for five minutes and then had to leave to deal with your runnings. Remember? When it hit me that you were gone, my high came crashing down."

Linvall sighed. He didn't need to hear this again, not now. Not ever.

"You cut me out of his life, Marce. You can't deny that. You were the one who refused to allow me to claim him as my son. You were the one who forced me to pretend that I was only his uncle. I used to be so angry with you for deceiving him, and depriving me of my child."

"But that is the exorbitant price you had to pay for the life you wanted to lead. In this life we must reap what we have sown. If you live by willy, you will die by it unless one day you are wise enough to put willy away and choose a better way of life. When Lacquan was born, I stood staring at this helpless creature I had brought into the world. He depended on me for his sustenance, his survival. I was forced to reconsider my life and where it was going. Our survival depended on me. From that moment on I began planning a course of action without you. I decided that I would shower all my love and attention on my beautiful baby boy, and that's what I did. If it wasn't for my parents, I may never have survived that period. They came all the way from Manchester to support me and welcome their grandson into the world. They helped me lift my spirits when I was at my lowest ebb. Ever heard of post-natal depression, Linvall? Oh, how I wish you could experience it just once."

'Well, too bad, I ain't never going to experience it,' Linvall was thinking, but didn't dare say. Not when

Marcia was on the warpath. She recalled how her mother had held Lacquan and beamed with loving approval, and how her father had embraced him and began whispering in his ear, in Arabic, the 'Athon', the Muslim call to prayer. It was a ritual all her father's children had experienced. But for the first time, she really understood what the words meant: 'God is the Greatest. There is no one greater than God'. All her life she had reiterated this message in Lacquan's ears, but he was a rebellious child. He was determined to do things his way. And for too long his way had not been God's way. She realised that he needed to redirect his life, but wasn't sure she could do it.

"So, it's your turn to have a go, Linvall. Because thanks to you, Lacquan is beginning to regard himself as something of a playa. Whatcha man, you can't let Lacquan be going on in dem ways. He picked his bad habits up from you in this house. You're his father, he'll probably listen to you. Meanwhile, you don't need me around, do you?"

Linvall shrugged his shoulders.

"If that's the way you want it," he accepted reluctantly. "So what are you going to be doing while I'm bringing Lacquan up?"

"I'm doing what I should have done a long time ago," she said. "I'm taking a holiday from you, Linvall. I've had enough of you for a while."

With that she picked up the house phone and dialled a mobile number.

"Oh hi, Amos . . . Yes, that's right . . ."

Marcia listened while Amos sweet-talked her down the line. She looked across at Linvall burning up beside her.

"Yes, I've decided to take you up on your offer," she said. "Yes, you can come around later with your jeep and help me move my things."

She signed off with a "Ciao!"

Linvall might have known that the detective had something to do with this. He made a resolve to win Marcia back. By hook or by crook. He would prove to her that the detective wasn't worth it. That she needed to give him another chance. He would even make Lacquan come correct, just to prove to her that he could really be a father to his son.

Easier said than done.

* * *

Ben tried as hard as he could to stick around while Gussie was sniffing around his woman. But, alas, business finally called him away to New York. Ben departed somewhat reluctantly, but still confident that Carmel wouldn't throw away all she had with him for a reckless fling with that black guy. He refused to believe that.

Who knows, Gussie may have hired a detective to keep watch over Carmel's place, because the moment Ben was climbing into a taxi with his suitcase, Carmel's phone rang and Gussie was inviting her over to his place for supper.

Shad spent the night with Gussie, in a manner of speaking.

They were now lying side by side on his bed, conversating, watching the early morning sunrays break through the window pane and sparkle in the river below. They had lain like this nearly all night long, with the only intercourse between them being an exchange of thoughts. Nothing more than the touching of fingertips, the seduction of a glance. She had fallen asleep for only twenty minutes, and as she slept he felt obligated to watch over her. He couldn't help but notice her erect nipples. He wanted to wrap himself around her, taste her passion deeply and devour her completely. But he had taken a solemn oath of 'No sex before marriage'.

He would later remember with sharp precision every second they spent together that night, and how her voice rose in an excited swirl as she told him of her dreams and aspirations and the other goings on in her subconscious. He looked into her eyes and with a voice soft and kind said, "You will have that yacht and the house on the Italian Riviera, too. And, of course, you can have all the diamonds you want. Did I mention that the jewellery business was very profitable at the moment? Especially the wedding and engagement ring aspect. Right now, I'm making more money than I know what to do with. If we two were one, all that was mine would be yours."

It was so easy to fall in love. One moment you're a playa, acting scrubs and playing pigeons, before you know it you taste cupid's nectar and there's nothing you wouldn't say or do to hit the mark. Exaggerating your earnings hardly seemed like a big whopper.

For Carmel, it was now a question of which was the best career move to make — Ben or Gussie?

* * *

Even though Linvall felt he had been doing the best he could as a father, the fact of the matter was that he had not been there for the first ten years of his son's life when Lacquan needed him most and, as a result, it was almost too late when he came back into the youth's life to mould him the way he would have wanted. He couldn't turn back the hands of time, but Lacquan would have turned out different if his father had been with him from day one. As proud as Linvall was of his son, he felt Lacquan would have made him even prouder had he been around in those formative years. But at the time it wasn't up to him. It was up to Marcia, who thought it better that her child never knew his own father.

Until this day Linvall had still never quite forgiven her for this. Okay, he had spent more time doing deals and trying to make a dollar than he had spent with his newly-born baby and Marcia, but he was doing it for her too. He had told her from the beginning that he was going to be rich. He didn't intend to struggle in life. He just needed her to take care of the baby and give him some space for a few years. He intended to make enough money to retire by the time he was thirty-five.

Everything was going smooth, according to plan. He just needed another five or six years and that one big break and he'd be done. Why couldn't Marcia just be cool and accept that?

But she wouldn't. Finally, one night, he took the decision that, well, if that's the way she wanted to play it, fine. It was going to spur him on to become even richer and more successful than she could imagine and he would make sure she regretted splitting up with him.

But she never regretted it. If anything, it was he who regretted not really knowing his son in those early years, not being there to watch him grow up.

Lacquan didn't come home until late that night, on account of the 287 Posse who ran the area, and were patrolling the streets from early evening until late. Lacquan's crew since he was in short trousers were the Brixton Bloods, and he never in his wildest imagination thought that his parents would subsequently move house to 287 territory on the other side of Coldharbour Lane — the wrong side as far as Lacquan was concerned.

But Linvall didn't want to hear all that. When he realised that Lacquan had sneaked up to his room just after midnight, he went up to confront him.

He hadn't been in Lacquan's bedroom in ages. The first thing he saw when he walked in was a large photo of Lacquan with his cousin, with the words 'Double Trouble' underneath. Johnny took note of it and kept it in his mind to ask his son what it meant exactly, what kind of trouble they were double of.

The next thing Linvall saw was Lacquan, relaxing on his bed, flicking through the pages of a copy of *Playboy.*

Linvall squeezed his son's ear and twisted.

"Dem t'ings will blind you, y'know," he said.

"Aaaaargh!" Lacquan cried with genuine pain. "Leave off, you're tearing my ear up."

"Well, if it's the only way to make you listen, because you seem to be very hard of hearing," Linvall told him. "What are you doing out this late? How many times have I told you that you're too old to be running around with a gang and that you have to get your head down and do well in school? But you still can't hear me. Well, all that is over, 'Quan. From now on, there'll be no more gangs, no more music. Until I see a major improvement in your school work, you'll come straight home from school — which you'll attend every day without fail — and you'll sit down and do your homework. On top of that, I want to see you learning ten new words a day, and I'll test you on them. Another thing, you'll get a paper round like I had to do when I was a kid. All this emceeing isn't doing you any good, you look too much like a gangbanger."

By now, Lacquan was literally crying. Emceeing was his life.If he couldn't go up on stage chatting lyrics, his life wasn't worth living.

"Good, cry if you want to," Linvall was saying. "How many times have I told you that me and you are not size? And that whenever I tell you something you must obey. 'Quan, why d'you have to go on with all this badness? I tell you to go to school and learn, you ignore me. I tell you to stay away from bad bwoys, you ignore me. Anything that smacks of my wishes you reject outright, cutting off your nose to spite my face. Being reckless. Ignoring sound advice."

"Well, my mum's always saying that I'm like my father and that I won't never amount to anything," Lacquan blurted through tears. "How do you think it felt to hear that? What do you think that did for my self-confidence? For years I wanted to ask you if she was right, but you weren't around, so I ended up believing her. She says she even had to get your father to show you the seriousness of the situation and how to take care of your son — that's how wotless you are. And, in case I didn't believe her that you were that wotless, she divided my wardrobe into two, with the fifty clothes she bought me on one side, and the measly one t-shirt and tracksuit bottoms that you got me for Christmas on the other."

Linvall couldn't believe what he was hearing from his son. Lacquan was only thirteen. Marcia must have been telling him all that nonsense from when he was at junior school. He looked at his son. There was no mistaking the resemblance between them. They shared the same almond eyes and angular cheekbones. Lacquan was going to be tall like his father and he certainly had the same dimpled smile. He was also going to be bad like his father, a real 'pickney with attitude'.

The next day, despite his son's protests, Linvall pulled him by the ear to the nearest barber's, to have his cornrows chopped off. As they strolled down Atlantic Road, side by side, Linvall suddenly realised that two young boys across the road were cussing bad in his direction. Lacquan, to his horror was cussing them back, as bold as day using the kind of words that Linvall used to get a spanking from his parents for. Lacquan stood at the kerb, his fists clenched in a stance that left the two boys with the red bandannas tied around their heads in no doubt that he was ready to fight them, any place any time, and that in fact this was as good a place as any and there was no time like the present.

Linvall eventually managed to tear his son away from the stand-off. He told the other two boys to clear off, waving his fists at them angrily.

"What was all that about?" Linvall asked sternly.

Lacquan looked up at him. "They called me a bitch," he said.

"That was it?" Linvall asked.

"Yeah," Lacquan said softly.

"So somebody called you a bitch, and you're going to fight them?"

"I've got my rep to think of?" Lacquan challenged.

Linvall sighed deeply. "For one thing, people have a right in this country to have that opinion about you and there isn't a damn thing you can do about it unless you want to get arrested for assault or manslaughter or something." He pulled Lacquan's ear again, he could see that this was going to be a long, hard road.

Indeed, Linvall hadn't got very far down that long hard road, when he heard a voice from behind call out:

"Linvall! Linvall, is that really you?"

He spun round to see the last person on earth he wanted to see. Lucy Fry.

"I was hoping I would bump into you, Linvall," she said. "That's the reason why I came all the way down to Brixton. I've got a surprise for you."

Linvall wasn't interested. He turned his back on Lucy and motioned to Lacquan to press on ahead. Lucy was trouble. Double trouble.

But Lucy was determined to have her say. She ran after Linvall, until she caught up with him. She grabbed him by the elbow and spun him around.

"Don't you turn your back on me," she shrieked in the crowded street.

If looks could kill, Lucy would be a dead woman. Because Linvall cut her one evil gaze and shook her arm off. He kissed his teeth and walked on.

Still, Lucy would not leave him alone. Again she caught up with him. This time, she didn't wait to be disrespected. She simply stuck her foot out from behind and tripped him up. Linvall went flying to the ground.

Lucy stood above him, defiant. She pointed at her pushchair in which sat a little mixed race baby of eighteen months or so, it was hard to tell.

"Linda, say hello to pappa," Lucy said.

"What?" Linvall could hardly believe his ears. His heart started pumping, hoping he didn't hear what he just heard.

"That's not a nice way to greet your daughter, Linvall. She's been dying to meet you. You could at least pretend that you were pleased to see her."

Linvall looked up at Lacquan, who had a sour look on his face. After picking himself up off the ground and dusting himself down, Linvall put a reassuring arm across his son's shoulders, but he was shrugged off.

"Look, 'Quan, let me deal with this nonsense. 'Cause that's all it is, y'hear? Go down to the barbers and I'll catch up with you in a minute after I've dealt with this woman, y'hear."

He skulked off, but not before giving Lucy one evil look.

Linvall waited until his son was well out of earshot before he started on Lucy.

"First of all, what the raas are you dealing with? You think you can just come up to me in the street when I'm walking with my son and start distressing me with some cock and bull story? I'm telling you, I don't appreciate dem way deh. And another thing, take that baby away and don't come here with that bull. Y'hear? Have you gone mad, woman? I haven't gone anywhere near you for years."

"Two years, to be precise," Lucy informed him. "If you've quite finished and pause to think about it, you'll work out that this is indeed, your child. Take a look at those eyes, look at that nose or that mouth, Linvall where have you seen them before. She's your spitting image, the only thing she gets from me is her intelligence."

Linvall had to admit that there was some similarity. Now his heart was pumping furiously, as he thought back on his brief relationship with Lucy Fry, back when he had been a trendy photographer and she was Head of Light Entertainment for Channel 5, the vital link that he needed in his wish for a TV vehicle to enhance his career. But that was back then. His life was different now. All he could think about was how he was going to keep this as quiet as possible from Marcia.

As usual, the barbershop was packed. The four barbers were snipping away at their normal leisurely pace when Linvall walked in. Linvall wanted to tell them to step on it, but stickers on the wall warned that: *Barbering is an art, it takes patience. If you're impatient, cut yourself.*

Finally, it was time for Lacquan to have his hair trimmed. The young barber motioned him to his empty chair. As Lacquan swaggered into position like Clint Eastwood, the ghettoblaster in the barber's salon exploded with the voice of the late great Peter Tosh:

You can't blame the youth
You can't fool the youth — of today

The barber fixed a white cloth around Lacquan's neck. Lacquan gave him full instructions of how he wanted his hair cut — how low, how gradual the fade, what kind of sideburns he wanted, and how he would allow the barber to put his signature on the back of his head if it was a good cut.

The barber started clipping away.

Linvall's thoughts were elsewhere, loving every

minute of it. On top of him she was going crazy, taking herself to the heights of ecstacy, then holding it. Stopping for a moment, pausing and then starting all over again with even more vigour than before. "You're going to be my undercover lover tonight," she whispered. He sighed with pleasure as he climaxed for the third time, a glazed look of surprised satisfaction on his face as he flopped limply on top of her. She had slammed the hell out of him. He was sore to the core and could barely walk.

With his father daydreaming and the barber clipping away, Lacquan took the opportunity to make some calls on his mobile.

Linvall may have been dreaming, but at the back of his mind he could hear his son threatening someone on the phone in a low voice. He just couldn't bring that thought to the foreground while his mind was on punnany.

"Lacquan, who are you talking to?" Linvall snapped to attention suddenly.

"Lacquan? Lacquan?" the barber said in astonishment. "Ah you dat? You name D.J. Pickney?"

Lacquan beamed a huge smile and nodded.

The barber slapped the young boy across the head and ran his razor right through the middle of his nice haircut, leaving him with almost no hair on top. Lacquan looked in the mirror and screamed with horror. His haircut had been well and truly mashed.

"It's you that made my sister pregnant, you raas you," the barber was saying as he slapped the bald patch on the youngster's head.

Linvall could hardly believe his ears.

"Lacquan, tell me that's not true."

Lacquan shrugged his shoulders like it was no big t'ing.

"I only pulled down my trousers once," he said innocently.

* * *

Unbeknown to Gussie, Carmel had made her decision. He had talked up his wealth so much so, and had even got into the habit of literally drenching himself in diamonds like Puff Daddy, items that he could borrow from his Hatton Garden jewellery shop, no problem. In short, he looked the business. Just the kind of man she was looking for.

But he wasn't the sort of man Millicent De Souza had in mind for her daughter to marry. No, not at all.

They were at his place one evening after only been dating for a few weeks, when he popped the question:

"Carm," he ventured, "why haven't you introduced me to your family?"

She couldn't honestly say that she was surprised, it was inevitable. They were having a great time together. Yeah, she had to admit it. All that wine and dining and being entertained. She remembered with sharp precision every minute they had spent together. It was so romantic. She was on top of the world whenever they were together, even if all they did was walk hand in hand along the Embankment with little more than the seduction of a glance and the touching of fingertips to amuse them. It seemed like they had spent a whole summer rediscovering the wonder of love.

And in all that time, Gussie had avoided 'getting it on', in fact, positively refused to. Like he was keeping it sizzling for her.

Oh boy, she have no idea what was on his mind. He had the urge all right. He wanted to pinch that tight behind and quiver inside her. But he wanted to do it right this time. No sex before marriage had become his mantra. He had learnt his lesson. He wasn't going to allow anything to jinx the relationship. He had told hardly anybody about her. He didn't want anyone to meet her or talk to her. That was the way he was going to keep it until that ring was firmly on her finger and they were declared man and wife, because he didn't want anybody mashing things up for him.

Once he had started lying about his true wealth, it seemed to get easier for Gussie. It was easy to play the millionaire lifestyle with the help of some creative accounting and a few credit cards. He was spending money he hadn't even made yet, showering Carmel with as much jewellery as she wished. There wasn't a thing he wouldn't do for her.

However, no matter how much he enjoyed time spent with her, not introducing him to her family was a big deal for Gus. Especially when one considered all the expensive dresses, shoes and jewellery that he couldn't resist buying for her.

"Is it that you're ashamed of me?" he asked, giving her that confused look she had come to know all too well.

She had a ready answer for that one.

Of course she wasn't ashamed of him. Shame had nothing to do with it. In fact, as she told him repeatedly, she was actually proud of him.

"Then what is it? Is it that you're ashamed of your family?" he persisted.

"Yes, that's it," she said, gratefully. "Once I introduce a man to my mother, the relationship always seems to take on a different, almost contrived dimension."

Gussie should have left it at that, and let the matter drop. But he persisted, until she started thinking about it constantly. Eventually she gave in

Carmel had invited Gussie to meet her mother for dinner at the Dorchester on Park Lane. Gussie had arrived, looking like a million dollars. The only thing that looked out of place was the haircut he sported, the type that you can usually read. He had even leased a criss looking Merc for the occasion. It was the first time he had ever been to the Dorchester, but he knew what kind of a hotel it was, and he didn't want to be outshone by all the billionaires that wandered through. This was the jet set crowd. But Gussie could hold his own. He looked trim, too. That much he was confident of. Since re-starting his regular workouts at the gym, nobody had dared to call him 'turbo belly'.

In the hotel foyer, men in expensive suits sipped from glasses of champagne while their girlfriends, hair braided and barely dressed in — even more expensive — clinging, revealing outfits, were purring beside them.

Carmel looked fabulous, too. "Wear that lovely sling-back, white dress," Gussie had suggested. "You look great in it."

He was right of course.

Gussie spotted Carmel's mother immediately. It had to be her. He noticed the woman looking at him across the restaurant as soon as they entered, almost undressing him with her eyes. Gussie paused like a film star, giving her a moment to catch her breath. He wanted to make a good impression on Millicent De Souza, he might as well start by giving her a long look at his good side.

Millicent spotted him immediately, too. Took an instant dislike. The next instant, visibly shocked when she saw his arm wrapped around her daughter's waist, she liked him even less.

Mother and daughter embraced in an affectionate 'welcome home' kind of way. Millicent was also turned out looking sharper than a razor. She must have been in her fifties, but looked ten years younger. In fact, Gussie was thinking, in a certain way she looked more attractive than her daughter.

Gussie approached Carmel's mother with love and respect, but he received no love and respect in return.

"You must be Mrs. De Souza," he said, but she ignored him.

Carmel hadn't told her mother about the new man in her life being black. Didn't think she needed to.

Millicent saw it differently. What on earth did Carmel think she was doing? She couldn't seriously be considering dumping Ben and all he had to offer, for what'shisname with the several pounds of vulgar jewellery on his fingers and hanging from his neck. He was clearly no serious contender for her daughter's hand. "This will all end in tears," she told her daughter. "You mark my words."

"I said you must be Mrs. De Souza," he repeated.

"How did you guess?" she asked, somewhat ironically.

"You look exactly alike," he said, turning from mother to daughter.

The answer, although genuine, left out specifics.

"What exactly do you mean by alike," Millicent asked.

Gussie came a bit closer. After some thought and further inspection he said, "The shape of your face is the same."

Mrs. De Souza nodded. "As is the shape of our feelings," she added mysteriously.

"I hope you don't mind me giving you this rose," he said, producing one seemingly out of thin air, but totally unexpectedly from behind his back, "but I just had to show it how beautiful you are."

It was a good line. One that he had picked up a while back from some Hollywood flick. It would have worked on any other woman, but not Millicent De Souza. She figured the rose was an attempt to soften her up. He handed it to her nevertheless.

"So, how do you like me so far?" Gussie grinned, sure that she was approving.

The Gussie that Millicent pictured before her, had little resemblance to the reality sitting opposite her at the dining table. He had no idea that Millicent saw no smiling, neatly-dressed character facing her. Had no idea that from her point of view he looked less handsome and less charming than he really was, and she couldn't understand how her daughter had fallen for him. Gussie couldn't in his worst nightmare have imagined that when Millicent looked at him what she saw was someone who resembled a homeless person. When she looked at his criss haircut and his sharp Yves St. Laurent suit and tie, all she saw was straggly hair and unkempt clothing. Far from hearing eloquence in his voice, she heard a boozy slurring of words and the sullen sucking of his teeth when he wanted to end a conversation. He needn't make the effort to impress her because, as far as she was concerned, he was a drugs dealer.

As they tucked in to their respective choices of dinner, Gussie continued joking. Worse, he was laughing at his own jokes. More out of nervousness than anything else. He told another joke. And another.

Millicent told a few good one liners of her own.

"I expect you have a room key to every hotel in town," she said to Gussie.

"I wish," he grinned leerily, not getting her drift. Still grinning, he turned to Carmel, while under the table he brushed her inner thighs with his knee. He looked into her eyes, asking permission to go further. Permission was not forthcoming.

When Gussie accidently spilled some wine on his jacket, Millicent piped up: "You're drunk. Be careful. Don't you have to return your suit to the store tomorrow?"

"I beg your pardon," he queried not quite grasping the gravity of the situation.

He wasn't blind, he could see a plastic smile when it presented itself, but he didn't want no cuss and quarrel. You get me? He was determined to stick around long enough to be recognised as a son-in-law in the making. Carmel was the woman of his dreams, and of such quality background that he was almost prepared to marry their cat just to get in the family.

The evening picked up with momentum as each event was to unfold. First, Carmel needed to powder her nose. She excused herself and went in search of the little girl's room, leaving Millicent and Gussie to get to know one another.

The silence was so loud it was deafening. Gussie looked into Mrs. De Souza's beautiful eyes and felt the chill of being ignored. He downed a glass of champagne quickly, felt it evaporate up his nose. His mind started playing tricks on him, teasing his imagination. He found himself looking at Millicent like he wanted to take her, make her, break her. Tame her. Like he wanted to know what shape her mouth takes when she comes. Yeah, he fancied her. Why not, she was good looking, nice. What was he to say? If the truth were to be told he wouldn't have minded giving it to her. It would have troubled him that he fancied her, but since he wasn't going to be getting the chance in this lifetime, he wasn't too bothered.

He picked up the breadbasket and passed it to Millicent. "Want a roll?" he asked innocently.

"If you mean do I want to have sex with you," she challenged, "the answer is most definitely no."

Gussie choked on the roll he was chewing.

Millicent gave him a cold stare.

"Carmel is out of your league," she said, "set your sights lower next time."

Since her husband's death, she and her daughters had had to make their way as three ordinary women trying to survive in a man's world.

"Look, I love your daughter, I've loved her from the very first time I set my eyes on her," Gussie began. He could see that Millicent was a protective mother and, quite understandably, wanted to make sure that Carmel had the very best. He wanted to reassure her that he would take care of her daughter, that he was a man with great ambition.

"Your daughter's tied a knot in my heart," he told her. "I love the ground she walks on. She must be a broom, 'cause she just swept me off my feet. No, I'm not drunk, I'm just intoxicated by her and the more I drink, the more intoxicated I become."

He knew what he meant, he hoped Millicent did also. He wished he hadn't drunk so much now. He had been knocking them back quicker than he realised. It was unbelievable how easy it was to down a bottle and a half of expensive white wine.

"Let me tell you," Millicent, unaccustomed to being frank about these matters, was uncharacteristically flustered. "You're not the first to try and win my daughter's hand, and you won't be the last. You've got nothing in common, so why don't you take what little pride you've got left and go and find yourself another woman. Because no way will you marry my daughter. No way. I warn you, I'm no pushover. What's mine is mine, I'll defend it to the full. Just because you see me looking nice and easy and I conduct myself discreetly, don't be fooled. There's also a different side of me that you don't know. If you want to play rough I can play rougher. If you want to get tough I can get tougher. You can huff and puff and blow in my face."

Meantime — and there was plenty of meantime — Gussie started wondering. Why was Millicent so disapproving about him? He had tried his uttermost to be civil and charming and the perfect prospective son-in-law. Yet, he could do nothing to please her.

It seemed she had a hang-up. A really big problem.

Yes, she did have a problem. For her, each encounter in life revealed something else about race. Connected, they showed the paradox of its relevance and irrelevance. What's skin got to do with it? It's at once absolutely important and altogether insignificant. It was insignificant where love was concerned, but it was the hard road to choose in life. You only had to glance at the *Sunday Times* Rich List to see that there were no black men in Britain who were eligible to marry her daughter. As far as Millicent was concerned.

Gussie was in shock and dismayed at her attitude. Though it was nothing to do with him, yet it was everything to do with him. When he finally realised what her problem was, Gussie decided to let her have it her way by informing Millicent of his 'true' ancestral background.

"Oh I'm all mixed up," he said, "we've got Chinese and Indian and a lot of white mix in our family. You wouldn't believe it, most of my family have got blue eyes and are so white you can barely see they're black."

"That may very well be," Millicent sneered unimpressed, "but what's the point of telling people that you are mixed with some other nationality when, clearly, your tight curly hair tells a different story."

Carmel returned from the ladies room, but now Gussie was bursting to go. He made his excuses and cut a quick retreat towards the gents, leaving mother and daughter alone at the table.

Millicent sighed. Her deep breasts surged. Carmel knew what was coming. Her mother was a domineering woman, her conscience, tormenting her.

"Everybody kept telling me this would happen. What went wrong?" Millicent asked. "How could it happen? Why didn't I see the signs?" She began to mourn her daughter as if she were dead. "No, not my daughter," she begged the heavens. Then turning to Carmel, she said, "You can walk out with me now, you know. Let's just go, leave him to pay the bill. You never have to see him again. You can call him later and tell him it's over down the phone line."

Carmel heard, but didn't want to listen. She knew it would happen. Knew that her mother would not approve of Gussie. That she would be floored by the suggestion that they intended to get married. Even her father, whom she had always thought of as the more understanding when he was alive, would not have approved.

Her mother belonged to the Caribbean colourtocracy. Had brought her daughters up with the knowledge that they would never have to work for a living because they were honey-coloured and butterscotch, and didn't have tippy toes or baby afros.

Millicent had been engaged in a crusade propelled by the frustration which she harboured towards her late husband for his betrayal from beyond the grave. Not a day passed when she didn't comment on black people and their lack of morality and values, not to talk of wealth. When she feared that her daughters might become attached to their darker skinned relatives and role models, Millicent cut them off completely from the black world. She had made it clear, even back then, that she expected her daughter to not make the same mistake as she had made by marrying somebody who was a darker shade than her. Seeing that Carmel was so light she could pass for white, Gussie wasn't going to stand much chance.

Carmel may have been light, but she was still not white, not like her sister Amy, to her mother's chagrin.

But not quite white isn't black, either.

After half a century of black immigration in the UK, Millicent had seen little sign of black economic achievement. Her late husband was an exception to the rule. From where she was sitting, however, it seemed like the black folks were skylarking. Why otherwise would they own little more than a bookstore and a couple of record stores and pattie shops? "Black people give up too easily," Millicent had often told her daughters. "So many members of the black community are content to conform to the lot they have been given in life. Take a look around you — both sides of the road are dotted with pitiful, able-bodied men and women who have allowed the winds of circumstance to blow them in every direction until they finally succumb to the devil in one of his many guises and, humiliated by poverty, simply drift along in life, hoping that something positive will turn up eventually, or at least that nothing negative does. No sparkle in their eyes. No hopes, dreams or aspirations."

What upset Millicent the most about the way her husband had died, was that he had left every penny to his mistress, leaving his own family near destitute, except for a house in Holland Park, which was currently rented out for income. The fact that J. Arthur De Souza's mistress was white didn't make it any easier for his wife to swallow. As she had nothing nothing against white people per se, Carmel turned her venom on her own people. She was hurt, very hurt and refused to let another black man hurt her.

"Mark my words, Carmel, that boy is poison," Millicent continued. She kissed her teeth. "He must have used some science to steal your heart and drive you right out of your mind. Because you're not thinking straight if you're even considering him as your fiancé."

Maybe Gussie had worked some science on her because, lately, Carmel been taking long hard looks at who she was becoming, and constantly asking herself what she really wanted out of life. She was coming up with answers like, a meaningful career, a loving family, a husband who would be both a spiritual and intellectual companion. She had always been close to her mother. At the same time, their relationship had been fraught with a conflict of expectations. Millicent expected certain things from her daughters, things which Carmel didn't want. Yet she wanted to be a daughter her mother could be proud of, but she also wanted to be a woman her child would be proud to have as a mother. All her life she had been running away from something, but now she wanted to create a space for herself in the world.

"Are you looking for Mr. Right, or Mr. Right Now?" she asked her daughter. "It seems to me that you can't make up your mind for yourself, dear. First Ben, then this fellow, whose name I can't bring myself to utter — Gassie — such a common name for a commoner, don't you think? Up to now you've been lucky in love, but you don't want to push it. In the game of life, jumping from one man to the other is a dangerous escapade. If you're not careful, you'll end up like a door knob, with everybody getting a turn. Look, dear, are you sure you can't patch things up with Ben? I'm sure it's not too late. As long as you get back in there before another woman comes along, you'll be his number one choice. Not a bad choice, if I might add. Otherwise I know several other nice rich single men. Let Gassie find some secretary to marry, that's about his level."

Gussie returned, still pulling up his zip as he sat down. Carmel got up immediately. She said she had a private phone call to make. She fished her mobile out of her leather handbag and wandered out to the hotel foyer.

"Your mum hates my guts," Gussie said.

Carmel shrugged her shoulders. "My mother is my mother, and she's very protective of me and of our relationship. She feels that I deserve more than second best."

"What's she got against black folk?" he asked.

"Oh, it's a long story," Carmel said. "I won't bore you with it. Suffice to say that negotiating my mother's ways and opinions continues to be one of the challenges of my intellectual life. To her, the world is black and white, end of story. Everyone has to choose which side they're on and stick to it. It more or less defines her relationships."

"So, where does that leave us?" Gussie asked.

"If you believe in what you're feeling," she said simply, "and you still want to marry me, then be prepared to work hard for it."

Millicent had only been gone a short while when she

returned, a mysterious smile on her face. She sat down. Gussie observed her nervously. There was something about her that gave him the heebie jeebies. She was one of those ladies who you couldn't easily decide if you liked her less as a person or as a woman. One thing was for sure, she was the living gorgon.

The problem about lying, is that you have to be careful not to believe your own hype. The only thing that Gussie could think of to get Mrs. De Souza to look at him in a favourable light, was to exaggerate his wealth. He knew these rich people, the only thing they ever respected was someone who was rich also. So he told her how rich he was and how much richer he was about to be.

Money talks. Since becoming a fantasy millionaire, Gussie had been living a completely different life in his mind, one that he wouldn't have imagined in all his years existed out there. His lifestyle now was light years away from the 'collective black experience'. In his daydreams, he was being invited to meet the Queen, the Prime Minister and an endless list of toffs ranging from knights of the realm to minor viscounts and barons. His beliefs had changed accordingly, to such an extent that the self-appointed 'policemen of black political correctness' regarded him a 'sellout'. An 'Uncle Tom'. But what did they know? As far as Gussie was concerned, they were just jealous.

No matter, as long as he was getting something out of it. This daydream believer floated into that elusive club of rich men and women known as 'the establishment'. He was being invited to all sorts of places where few black men could get to. He had even been invited to Buckingham Palace to meet the Queen and all. Who would have thought it? Now that he was rich and was playing the game, as it were, it seemed like nothing could stop him. Nothing, that is, except his baby mother. He had still not mentioned his two kids out of wedlock to Carmel. He had kept meaning to, but he never ever found the right opportunity. He was going to mention it tonight but meeting Millicent De Souza had changed his mind about that. She would eat him for breakfast if she found out. So he resolved to keep it a secret for ever.

"Yes, I'm making so much money, it's incredible," Gussie was saying. "It's like it's growing on trees."

Millicent listened. As he spoke, she seemed to be staring at his mouth. It was quite disconcerting. He wondered if he had a bit of food on his chin and she was pointing it out very subtly. He was embarrassed. He tried to brush it off blindly, but he didn't seem to be able to get rid of it no how no way, and she continued staring, keeping an eye on him.

"By the way," she said suddenly, "how many times have you been married?"

Gussie wasn't expecting that one. The question hit him in the stomach like a bullet, and he recoiled visibly. How did she know? What had she found out? Had she found out anything? Who was that phone call from?

"W-w-what do you mean?" he stuttered.

"Come, come now. Don't tell me you've forgotten

about your marriage?"

No, he hadn't forgotten. How could you forget something like that? Carmel who was now cutting her eye at him. He didn't want to tell the truth, yet he didn't want to get caught in another lie.

"Oh, *that* marriage . . ."

Carmel had to restrain herself.

"Oh *what* marriage?" she asked.

"I was going to tell you," Gussie said, "I really was."

"And what about your kids, you know, the twins? Or have you got more kids elsewhere?" Millicent continued.

Gussie was astounded. She did know something, no doubt about it.

"Kids?" Carmel asked, with anger in her eyes.

Yes, kids. Gussie had dreaded having to tell Carmel about his kids and had done a good job in conceal it until now.

Wriggle as he might, Gussie couldn't find a way out. Millicent probed ever deeper.

"I can't say I was surprised when he discovered the truth. Anyway, I'll try not to take up any more of your time than I need to, but would you mind telling me, I'd appreciate it, when all of your money is spent on your kids — as it should be — how are you going to have any money to spend on my high maintenance kid?"

Yes, Millicent De Souza was the living gorgon. When Gussie looked close, he could see the circles under her eyes. When he looked even closer he realised they weren't circles, but three sixes.

Gussie had nowhere to hide, nowhere to run. All he could think of was to tell Carmen's mother, "Clean your own backyard before you start thinking about a next man's."

Millicent laughed. "That's the most foolish thing you've said since I met you."

* * *

There was going to be hell to pay. Linvall knew. When Marcia found out that her thirteen-year-old son was about to become a father, he would get the blame. She would talk about the bad example he had set as a father and he would have to take it. She would never let him hear the end of it.

He still couldn't get his head around the fact that he would soon be a grandfather. As far as he had known, Lacquan had never seen a naked body, except in movies. How was he to know otherwise?

Linvall was only now beginning to realise that, despite his thirteen years, his son had grown up fast. It was no easy thing trying to keep him in check. On his own to do the job, Linvall began to realise what it must have been like for Marcia all those years, because Lacquan was a real handful.

They should have named him Patrick, because the boy was, quite simply, a trickster. When Lacquan was supposed to be at his cousin Darren's house, for instance, he was never there. Linvall would ring up only to find out that Darren had told his parents that they were going to be staying over at Lacquan's. In reality, they were having a good time together at some rave or other. Then Lacquan would sneak home after five in the morning with no suitable excuse.

Learning ten new words a day hardly seemed relevant now. Lacquan was acting like he didn't have any respect for his elders and was already talking about how he was a big man now and had to earn money to take care of his pickney. He even had the nerve to put up his fist to his father, like he was ready to take him on for the world heavyweight title.

Linvall was dismayed. Marcia was going to skin him alive unless he managed to turn his son around. Sure, he had to give Lacquan some slaps to the neckback for such impertinence, but he knew that ultimately all the ear pulling and clouts round the earhole were achieving little. The pain was going in one ear and out the other. Lacquan took all the blows like a bad bwoy. Like he wasn't supposed to cry, no matter what. Like he was just supposed to fold his arms and be even more rebellious.

"Yeah, you're right," Linvall told him, "you're a big man now, you can make your own decisions, but seeing that you've started to act childish I have to start treating you like a big child."

6/WHO IS SHE, AND WHAT IS SHE TO YOU?

a) 'The Healing Stroke'
With the shaft resting on the belly, the hand closest to the feet cups the balls. The heel of the palm of the other hand glides up and down the underside of the shaft.

b) 'Tap Dancing'
Place the palm of your hand on her mons (the mound where her pubes are), and rest your fingers lightly on her vaginal lips. Rest your thumb on her opposite thigh. Lightly but firmly press your palm onto her mons and begin to move your hand in a tiny circular motion. You palm should not slide too much over her skin during this process. Instead, her skin should move underneath it. Repeat this process until you have done ten circles. You then raise your fingers and lightly tap her vaginal lips about once a second until you have given her ten taps. Please note that these are light taps, not spanks. They shouldn't hurt. After giving the taps, rest your hand for five to ten seconds. Then repeat the circles, then repeat the taps, then rest again, then repeat the circles.

If you want a satisfying sex life, you will NEVER fake it.

It is a blow to any woman to discover that she no longer has what it takes to turn her man on. Especially if she's has hit thirty. She'll blame it on herself and the passage of time.

Beres had been faking orgasms for weeks by the time Caroline found out. It intrigued her to find an empty condom after their last session, even though he had cried out for several minutes with unrestrained ecstacy. She faired the truth in her suspicions. As far as she was concerned, there was no smoke without fire. Why would Beres be faking it, unless she didn't turn him on any more? But how could he have gone off her so quickly? She who had always been able to turn him on so easily. She looked in the mirror for an answer. If you look long enough, you'll definitely find some. For the first time she noticed a couple of grey hairs on her head. For the first time she noticed the lines forming on her neck and the bags under her eyes. She was definitely thirtysomething and getting older. Yet, still, she couldn't accept that she was losing her touch, that old black magic that she had always had.

Determined to prove that she still had it in her, she was waiting for Beres when he came home that evening, with the look of desire in her eyes.

Beres knew what was coming. But he didn't want to. He had made up his mind that he would swallow his pride and crawl on his knees and do anything he had to to get Sonia back. Meanwhile, there was no point in carrying on faking it with Caroline. The moment had come. He had to tell her straight, that they should get a divorce and remain good friends. He would pack his things and move out as soon as possible, otherwise he might end up right back in her bed nibbling her ear. That's what he was going to say. But he didn't get a chance before she fell on her knees, pulled down his zip, and reached out and gripped the shaft of his already stiff piece and, with her face between his legs, proceeded to give him a once in a lifetime blowjob.

Beres should have cried out and begged her to stop, but it felt too good. Judging from his soft moans, whispered like a prayer, and the smile on his face, he was in a place of erogenous stimulation. She teased as she tasted, pushing all the right buttons, arousing all his senses, trying her best to blow his mind. She chewed her food slow. Sipped and savoured. She licked him up slowly, and then all the way down fast,working his pleasure zone like it had never been worked before.

He had never imagined that oral sex was anything more than in and out, in and out. Something about the way she licked her lips brought out the freak in him and made him believe that he could finally enjoy a climax with her. He could feel his soldiers coming up, marching as to war.

He moaned a little louder. Caroline felt the shudder from one thigh to the other. She looked up. In Beres' glittering wet eyes she could read the words 'I eat, too.'

No, no, no. That wasn't what Caroline wanted. Another time maybe. Tonight, the pleasure was all hers. Tonight, she wanted to sip from his endless fountain without missing a single drop.

He held her hand while kissing her neck. With his other hand he stroked her behind. He felt weak in the knees. It didn't take long before he started gasping.

"I'm cuuummmmmming!" he cried with surprise, "I'm finally cuuuuuuummmmmmiiiing!"

A smile spread across Caroline's face. That's what

she wanted to hear. Unfortunately for the neighbours n the other side of the street, they had to hear it too.

"I-I-I-I-I-I'm cuuuuummmmmmmming!"

It was close, but not close enough. Beres did feel his soldiers rushing forth, but just before they poured out in their millions, they screeched to a halt, turned around, and made their way back. That was the only way he could describe it, because that's exactly how it felt.

But Beres couldn't fake it this time. Caroline awaited the outpouring of ecstacy, but waited in vain. After another ten minutes or so of the most sensual work with her mouth, she took his piece right out and began rubbing it against her mound. Her panties were still on but now she lifted herself allowing him to caress the lips of her veggie with his hard-on.

"Push," she said, "I want you in me."

He did as he was told, slid in a little slowly, feeling the warmness and the wetness — hot and slippery, the way he liked it. It was much sweeter than honey. He gave a little push. Determined to make his body sing, she grabbed him by his seed and started rubbing.

Sure enough, his body sang such a sweet melody. They got a little motion going in smooth, complimentary syncopation, the spicy aroma of their bodies intertwined.

The pelvic movements gained in intensity.

"How do you want me?" he gasped, "up high or down low? I want you to tell me what you want."

She shook her head. It wasn't about what she wanted. Not tonight anyway.

"Put it anywhere you please," she replied.

So he flipped her over on all fours and pulled up to the bumper, ass all up in the air, his chest against her back. He let his inhibitions loose as the feelings started to surge. Then he went down on his knees, her legs on his shoulders. Two bodies melting into a sexy sexual chocolate glaze. Touching the deepest part of her with sensual thrusts, he put his lips to her toes. She shouted with pleasure, just because she knew how much it turned him on to hear her scream with delight. Seconds later he was ready to blow his load, he was sure of it.

"This time it's for real," he cried out.

Yes, she could feel it in his hands as he gripped her tightly with his hands on the back of her head. She could see it in his eyes, feel it in his thighs and in his toes. This time it really was for real.

Unfortunately it wasn't.

By now Caroline was facing defeat. After a bit, she moved took his piece in her mouth again. It was semi-erect, but she fixed that quickly. Try as hard as she could, however, she failed to elicit from him that elusive climax.

It was hopeless. Caroline finally gave up and turned to Beres for an explanation.

"What's the problem?" she asked. "Is it something to do with me? Am I not fulfilling all your fantasies? How come you're not able to come?"

"I don't know," Beres said. He looked away, highly embarrassed. I don't know why, I'm just not able to reach orgasm."

"I know what you're feeling inside," she said despondently.

Beres wondered how she could possibly know. But he said nothing. Who feels it knows it.

But Caroline did know.

"Look, I said, I know. I know what you were thinking in the midst of our pleasure ride. Your ex-wife's friend, Grace, called me up this afternoon. She told me everything."

Beres could have collapsed on the spot.

"Grace? What did she tell you?"

"You know, how you're still in love with your ex. And how you're trying to get back with her."

Beres felt the palpatations in his heart. If he had come clean and told her himself it would have been so disrespectful, but to hear it from somebody else made him look like bad.

"I was going to tell you . . ." he began.

"Sure, sure. Anything you say." Caroline clearly didn't believe him.

She sounded pissed off. He couldn't blame her.

"No, really."

"I can't do this anymore, Beres, I am not your consolation prize."

She had every reason to be pissed off. It had pissed her off when Grace had phoned. Why would some woman you didn't even know go to all the trouble of getting your phone number and calling you to let you know that when your man is making love to you, he's really thinking about his ex-wife? Caroline may have been a lawyer by day, but when a woman gets that pissed off she loses all sense of reason and decides that she's going to get even. Or at least prove that her hot stuff is more irresistible than her rival's.

Why do women do that? Especially middle class women who claim to know better? It would have been more reasonable to simply kick Beres to the curb, but something deep down was egging Caroline on, against her better judgment, to prove that hers was the sweetness that Beres could not resist. Unable to prove it, she decided to kick him to the kerb after all. She went around the flat and threw out every item that belonged to him. Despite his protestations, she didn't want him in her home a moment longer.

* * *

Despite all his new millions, Johnny liked nothing better that to surround himself with the fellas he knew before he had money. In particular, Linvall, Beres and Gussie.

It was getting harder and harder to link up with them nowadays, because since going underground Johnny wasn't always able to make their regular Sunday night link ups. However, this was one Sunday he could make it.

They had hooked up at a private men's club on the Finchley Road. As the jukebox played away in the background and nude table dancers jigged their *thangs* beside them, the four friends settled down to the best champagne in the house. All compliments of millionaire

Johnny.

"So what have you been up to, Johnny?" Gussie was asking. "I haven't seen you since nineteen long time."

"Yeah, you know how it go — up and down, up and down. Or to put it another way, I've been putting the lash on this woman, but I don't know if I'm going to be putting the lash on her much longer, to tell you the truth. I'm getting tired of her."

"Well, Johnny, if you're not going to lash her, give her to the deputy nuh," Linvall suggested.

"You sure you can handle any woman that I've put the lash on?" Johnny retorted. "Linvall, go back ah school, man. Learn to lash it haaaard! Because, believe me, women pretend that they're looking for the sensitive and sincere kind of man with a good job, good education, good manners, good upbringing and a modicum of conversational skills, when what they really want is a man who is bad, mad and wicked in bed."

Johnny was on good form, entertaining his friends.

"Here's one more thing to add to my ever-increasing list of mistaken beliefs I've held about women throughout my life," he was saying. "I used to believe that the moment a woman stepped into a church, she became rigid and frigid and ugly, too. But how wrong can one man be? You see, back when I was still a virgin, I couldn't see much difference between a crucifix and a chastity belt. In my mind, if a woman was wearing the one, it was a sure bet that she was tightly strapped into the other, and like a vampire the very sight of that cross would make me fall back in horror."

The four friends burst out in laughter, causing everybody else in the place to be to turn around and see what was up.

Johnny continued.

"But I was wrong. How was I to know that a crucifix was as good as a nod and a wink and a come on? Back then I used to think that God was the bloke who always came between me and my desperate attempts to shed my school nickname of 'Richard Branson'. You get me? Back then I thought that church was where thirtysomething women turn for refuge when their man's left them and they're looking for solace in the faith. How wrong can a guy be? Church gals are bad, mad and wicked inna bed, trust me, and there's seven of them for every man. Typical, innit? It's the ones who went to strict convent schools who are always first to have their blouses up over their shoulders, bras off, slacks down around their knees, and panties bunched around their thighs. I tell you no lie."

"So how's this keeping a low profile going on? Haven't the CSA caught up with you yet?" Beres asked.

Johnny smiled arrogantly and cracked, "Man, you ain't heard? They've given up trying to track me down, I'm too good for them. They even sent a detective after me and everything, but you know how it go: 'they seek him here and they seek him there, the CSA seek him everywhere, is he in heaven or is he in hell, that damned elusive Johnny Pimpernel'."

Maybe it's true that oysters put lead in a man's pencil

(for they had each swallowed a dozen each), or maybe it was just all the naked table dancers around them, but each of the friends was feeling aroused. Fortunately, none of them knew what was going on between the others' legs nicely tucked beneath the table.

Beres had been outraged when Johnny suggested that they should go to nude bar.

"Would you want your woman to do laptop dancing?" he had asked.

"No," Johnny replied, "but I don't mind watching somebody else's woman do it. Anyway, it's not like it's an orgy or anything, it's very respectable. You've got to be three feet away from the women when they dance."

"Three feet away!" Beres had cried out. "Three feet? No man, if I'm paying that kind of money I want to see everything close up, man. Tight. You know what I mean?"

Johnny knew exactly what he meant.

"So I take it you'll be coming after all, then Beres."

With Linvall and Gussie, it was no problem. Convincing them to go was easy.

"Spend the night at a table dancing club," they had both said, "why didn't I think of that?"

"It seems to me that the fundamental problem between fellas and females will never be resolved," Linvall was saying. By now he had drunk three too many glasses of champagne, and he had noticed one of the table dancers across the room giving him the eye. "Quite simply, women want a man, and not just for Christmas, but for life. Guys, on the other hand . . .

Some guys will look at you and say that in fifty years of marriage they have never been unfaithful to their wives. In other words, in fifty years of marriage they have never been caught being unfaithful to their wives. Take a look at any married couple and you'll see that the man doesn't want to be in a monogamous relationship. Marital disputes, separations, divorce and arguments are basically a cry for understanding from the man that he would like to go out and try a slice of new veggie. It leads to stress otherwise, when men aren't getting new sex. I know this bloke who ain't had so much as a sniff, let alone a bite of the cherry, for years."

Linvall agreed.

"Women simply don't understand what men do, and really it's their problem not mine. They think it's perverse, it isn't. Men are different from women. They need different things. That's al] there is to it. If a woman can't accept it, then tough."

Gussie nodded.

"Women don't seem to appreciate a good thing when they have one. In the old days, the girls used to say that I was boring. Just because I spent all my time working, none of them were interested in me. They preferred to go after all the bad boys. But now that they're a few years older and wiser and know what life is all about, suddenly I'm Mr. Reliable and the girls are rushing me. I'm telling you, I can't cope with the rush right now."

The only black dancer in the house came with more champagne. From the look on their faces, none of the four men would have declined an offer. Even Beres.

The four friends said their 'pleases' and 'thank yous' to her. She in turn was pleasant and polite to them. Simple stuff which makes the world go around a lot more pleasantly. But they watched her reaction when the buppy on the next table slapped her naked behind and barked "give me a brandy" at her. She in turn was equally curt and barked back at him.

Then there was the embarrassing spectacle of the white manager of the establishment telling the black man to behave himself and to treat his staff respectfully. Fortunately common sense prevailed and the man soon realised that apologies were in order.

The four friends kept a dignified air of distance from the man. Shook their heads in disbelief at just how little bloody class some black Brits had.

"A lot of us don't know how to behave and haven't a clue what good manners are," said Gussie. "Why do some people seem to have such a big problem with 'please' and 'thank you'? All of us deserve good manners and respect so why is it such a big problem to give it? Even among those who should know better, a lack of social sophistication is embarrassing by its absence. For example, last year, at a buffet dinner for black professionals that I attended, a large number of people shamed themselves by trying to rush the food rather than forming a dignified queue. I couldn't believe it. If the supposed black British professional classes don't know how to behave, then I wonder if I should expect any better from Joe Public. 'Manners maketh man' is how the expression goes but, unfortunately, too many of us seem to think that the word 'manner' is something to do with your local neighbourhood. Even when the dinner was done and you attempted to try and get your vehicle out of the car park, there were more examples of pig ignorance and general bad attitude awaiting you. Instead of letting the traffic flow, everyone wants to be ahead of the next man with the result that all the traffic comes to a grinding halt. If it's not guys stopping their cars and creating a two mile tailback so they can chat to their spar, it's someone turning their motor around in the worst possible place and causing a road block."

"It's easy for you to say them kinda things, Gus," Johnny chipped in, "because you're so far away from what ah really gwaning in the black community today. It's like you and your buppie friends have all turned white or something. Check out the real deal, what's happening on the streets. Check out the conspiracy business, man."

"The only conspiracy I can see is lazy black men conspiring to distress things for the rest of us. It's all about not giving a damn about your fellow man, and if he's a black person then that means you gotta give him even more disrespect. Have we bought into the belief that your fellow black man or black woman is not worthy of any courtesy or consideration any more? I get tired of hearing people complain about how white people treat them. It seems to me that we need to get our own house in order and start to treat each other with respect before we start winging on about others.

After all if we can't respect ourselves how the hell can we expect others to do so?"

It wasn't the right occasion to get heavy and serious about the state of the black community, however, and pretty soon the conversation reverted back to sex. Especially when another naked woman turned up at their table to jiggle and wiggle.

"Wedding rituals and religious controls can't keep you from wanting new sex," Linvall was saying, ruing the fact that he couldn't seem to get any illicit sex of his own, no matter how hard he tried.

"By the way I'm getting married again," Gussie said.

His spars thought he was having a laugh. After the mess he had already made of his life in the marriage department, they all assumed that Gussie would stay well clear of all that stuff and remain a bachelor.

But Gussie wasn't kidding. He was deadly serious. He kept assuring them that he had at last found the right woman, and from the way he said it, it looked as if he really had found the woman he had been waiting all his life to marry.

"I still can't believe it," he continued with tears in his eyes. "I just can't believe it, but it's all real."

When his friends asked what the woman was like he smiled and joked, "Leggy, big tits, you know the score."

Even Johnny could tell that that was not what had really attracted Gussie to this woman. Gussie had already learned his lesson of going after women with long legs and big tits from his previous failures, and wasn't about to make that same mistake again.

"Okay," Johnny began, advising his friend, "if you're crazy about this woman, go ahead and marry her. I haven't met her, and personally, I would have liked to have given you a second opinion before you made your big decision, after all I am your spar and, after all, what are good friends for if it isn't so that you can come and ask each other to give a potential wife the once over? I am your spar, I've known you long enough and know by now the kind of woman who would be right for you and the kind of woman who would be wrong for you and, frankly, if you had come up to me and asked, I would have gladly given you my expert opinion. However, it seems from that lovesick look on your face that I am too late and that you wouldn't listen to me even if I had some observations to make. So, the one thing I would ask you to consider very well — take heed of my superior knowledge of the female species, trust me, I've been giving free consultations for years — before you tie that wedding knot, make sure that she knows where you're coming from, and spell out in great detail all the rules and regulations of married life, and play her into commitment and an air-tight mouth-to-mouth agreement. You don't have to be a rocket scientist to know that if you heed my lessons, you'll stay in control. Satisfy your woman regularly and there'll be no reason for her to stay up half the night awake."

The others nodded in agreement. It was sound advice. The kind of advice every man should heed. Even a blind man in the fog could see that.

7/DO RIGHT WOMAN, DO RIGHT MAN

a) 'Fire'
Rub the shaft between both palms, as if rubbing two sticks together to create fire. Come on, baby, light that fire.

b) 'Fingers on the Hood'
Given how the clitoral area is sensitive, you don't want the rough skin of your fingers rubbing across it. Gently push and pull on the clitoral hood and labia when first touching a woman's genitals. Using the lips as leverage can provide pleasing stimulation without painful friction.

There's always a woman out there who will tempt a man. It all depends on the man whether or not he will allow himself to be tempted and how strong he is otherwise.

Gussie woke up the morning of his wedding with a splitting headache. He couldn't remember anything about his stag night. Not the booze, the antics nor the woman lying in bed beside him.

"Woman! Help," he screamed despite himself, jumping up and leaping out of bed. He was naked. He grabbed the sheet from the bed and wrapped it around himself, exposing her to the world.

She was naked as well. She looked fabulous. Just his type. A voluptuous body full of all the curves and pouting, enticing lips, a nice round behind which no man could have possibly resisted. Surely not.

Admiring him with that seductive smile of hers, she crooked her finger and beckoned him towards her. He found himself, despite himself, being drawn to her. As in a dream. As if he was a robot climbing on top of her and sliding his head down between her legs.

"Nooooo!" he screamed, waking himself up with a jolt, sitting bolt upright in the bed. *Phew.* Thank goodness, it was only a dream, a nightmare. The kind of thing he didn't need happening on his wedding day.

He rolled over in the bed.

"Aaaaaaaagh!" he screamed as he felt the firm round juicy flesh of the woman lying naked next to him. This wasn't a dream after all? This was real.

As far as Gussie could remember, he had cancelled the stag night when he got wind that his spars were planning a real orgy of debauchery for the evening. He had only intended to have a quite drink at his private members club in Soho. When he realised that they intended to compromise him, he had backed out. Now that he had managed to win the woman he wanted to spend the rest of his life with, he couldn't afford to risk everything with typical stag night antics. He had already made his mistakes and they had cost him dear. He had one failed marriage and two kids by another woman to account for. He didn't want any more accidents in his life. That's why he had taken it nice and slow with Carmel. That's why he had avoided the sex issue, preferring to try out the old fashion ways where a man courted a woman for several months and delayed the sex thing until they got married. All the lust he had for Carmel (and there was plenty of it) had been saved for tonight, when he would make up for lost time. The wedding night was supposed to be special and indeed it would be. He had waited all this time and the last thing that he needed was to ruin it all at the final furlong by jumping in bed with some woman he didn't even know. Who was she and, most importantly, did they sleep together?

He didn't even have to ask her that.

"You're one of the best lovers I've ever had," she purred. "And believe me, I've had several!"

"Oh my lord!" Gussie cried out. What had he done? Oh Lord, what had he done? "Woe is me, woe is me . . ." he bawled, wringing his hands.

"Listen, you don't have to get upset about it," the woman said. "Okay you were the absolute best, if that will make you feel better. You were so good, that I'm looking forward to the next time you'll do me the honour."

That made Gussie bawl out in tears. Any other time it would have been a compliment, but the last thing he needed now was to bone some other woman on the eve of his wedding and to have her thinking that he was so good she wouldn't mind keeping this t'ing going for a while.

Now he knew what he had done, what was he to do? He had to get to the church on time.

"So," the woman continued, "when exactly can I see you again?"

Gussie's heart pumped, yes he knew that that was

coming.

"I don't know what you're talking about," he said, putting on a macho thing, to scare her away by showing her how mean and horrible he could be. "I only bone women once, I've got too much sweetness in me," he said, "there are too many other women in the queue waiting to get some of my brown sugar . . ."

"Charming," she said. "Did anybody ever tell you that you were damn outta order?"

Gussie wasn't listening, he was admiring her gorgeous hips and the patch of black triangle below her belly button. She must have been delicious he was thinking. If only he could recall any of it. If only he could have one more quick go so that he had some memory to remember her by.

Damn! What was he thinking. Thoughts like that were dangerous. He had to get rid of this woman, get her off his case.

"Lady, I don't know who you are, but I'd appreciate if you took your fine ass outta here and let me get on with my life . . ."

He had to be cold to be kind, quite simply.

The woman wasn't taking that for an answer, though. She picked up the bedside lamp and threw it at him. Luckily he saw it coming and ducked. It went crashing into the wall in a thousand pieces.

"Next time, I won't miss on purpose," the woman said and jumped off the bed in a huff.

She seemed to know her way around his flat pretty good, and went to the bathroom slamming the door behind her.

Gussie started to panic. He had loads of things to do. He looked at the clock, it was just gone eight o'clock. He still had time. He looked down at his manhood, the stench of sex was rising up. Damn.

* * *

It was the black society wedding of the year. Gussie had borrowed heavily to have the funds to be able to bring the crème de la crème of the community together to show the world that they had arrived.

Traffic in the surrounding streets had been brought to a crawl as new registration Beemas, Mercs and Lexuses arrived from every direction, honking loud horns, all looking for a parking space close to the church.

It was the first time in years that Linvall had seen his son in a suit. Hired, of course, but at least he had managed to get Laquan to wear it. It was no easy feat. Lacquan seemed determined not to look like "one of them Uncle Toms" (Lacquan's words not Linvall's).

It was one thing to get Lacquan in the suit, it was another thing to make him wear it in public. Linvall literally had to drag his son to the church, finally giving in to his Lacquan's insistence on being allowed to wear a pair of dark shades, on account of his 'rep'.

As they made their way to the wedding, Linvall passed judgement on Lacquan's recent misdemeanours, having waited two weeks for psychiatric reports before he delivered his final verdict.

In his defence, Lacquan had said that he had been unlucky enough to get his girlfriend Kimini pregnant the very first and only time he had ever had sex. Both he and Kimini (they later discovered to their joint amusement), thought that they were giving in to the other's pressure to "do the deed". Each had gone into the situation reluctantly but had put their trust in the other who, they each thought, had more experience and could teach them a thing or two that day. So they had both cut school and spent the afternoon in Lacquan's bedroom one day when Linvall was downstairs watching television.

"You get me?" Lacquan had asked his dad.

Linvall had nodded, or at least he thought he understood his son's account of the series of events.

But Lacquan's "You get me?" didn't refer to the series of events. It was a challenge to Linvall. As sharp as ever, Lacquan had picked up on the fact that his dad was going to be deadmeat when his mum found out that the deed was actually done literally under his father's nose. He wanted to make it clear that, depending on how lenient Linvall treated him, he would consider omitting certain details out when his mum demanded to hear the whole truth and nothing but.

"It was my first time," Lacquan had said proudly, "but it won't be my last. It was great. I didn't know what to do at first. I mean, I've seen all the pictures in the dirty magazines, but what's the use of looking if you don't know what they mean."

"Yes, all right, Lacquan. No need for the details," Linvall had shuffled his feet uneasily. He didn't know what good it was going to do, but he had to impose some punitive sanctions so that Lacquan wouldn't think that making a girl pregnant was painless.

"For a start, I'll be keeping your pocket money to teach you a lesson."

Lacquan had shrugged his shoulders.

"Like I need it. Big deal. I can make more money in a week than you give me in a year."

"Not any more you can't. Because you'll be too busy studying with every spare minute available. Look how long it's taken to get you to think that it's worth putting something in your head, yet all you're interested in is jumping and whining. You've got a lot of catching up to do on all the school work you've missed. Until that's done, there'll be no more 'skin up batty'."

Again, Lacquan had shrugged. Like he cared.

"I'll still be collecting royalties for months yet," he had said defiantly.

"In that case you can start paying rent."

"Rent? Rent? What are you talking about rent? When I was a boy you didn't ask me for rent, so what are you trying now that I'm a man?"

"I don't care what you say, if you're old enough to get girls pregnant, you're old enough to pay rent."

"You get me, though?"

No, Linvall didn't get him, though. "As for piercing your nose," he continued, "and that tattoo you've been begging me to let you have, you can forget it. And you can tell all your friends that you won't be going on that trip to Jamaica with them in the summer holidays. Because while they're basking in the sun, you'll be back here in summer school."

If Lacquan was a little older, he would not have stood for all this nonsense. He would have simply told his dad to stuff it and packed his bags and left home. That tattoo and the ring through his nose were vital components to his 'rep'. Though, not vital enough at the twilight age of thirteen when you are almost ready to leave home but not quite. The holiday was another matter. He would rather die than miss the holiday of a lifetime in the Caribbean with his best friends.

All Lacquan could do for now was make it clear to his father what slant he was going to have on the subject when his mother found out about it.

"Don't you think that you should take care of your own business instead of trying to clean a next man's yard. As I remember, you got that white woman pregnant. You wait until mum finds out. You don't have a leg to stand on. I mean, you haven't exactly set a good example, have you?" Lacquan said.

Linvall got the message loud and clear. Laquan fished his house keys out of his pocket and handed them to his father.

Linvall looked at the keys. The ear pulling and the slaps on Lacquan's neckback didn't seem to have worked. If it was up to him, he would let Lacquan find his own way in the world, he wouldn't even lose any sleep over it. But he knew Marcia wouldn't take too kindly to him 'throwing' his son out of the house, because that was the spin she would put on it.

"Pssss! Pssssst! Linvall!"

Linvall spun round surprised to see his rival in love dressed in a flash white suit, like a black John Travolta in *Saturday Night Fever*. He frowned. Why did he have to come? Not having told his friends about the stress and quarrel in his relationship, Linvall couldn't blame Gussie for inviting Marcia, and everywhere that Marcia went, the detective was sure to follow."

"Hey man, how are you doing, I've been looking for you everywhere," Amos said. "Listen, do me a favour, if Marcia asks, I was with you last night."

"What?!"

"Whatever happens, I was with you last night," he said more urgently.

Linvall still didn't get it. So Amos spelled it out.

"If your wife speaks to you, we went out for a drink last night, you and I, and I couldn't make it home, so I stayed at your place!"

Linvall couldn't believe what he was hearing. Amos needed two serious slaps. This bloke had the nerve . . .

He shook his head in refusal.

"If you want to go out and have affairs behind my woman's back, that's your business," Linvall said, "but don't go dragging me into it."

"You know what they call that, don't you? Penis envy."

"I beg your pardon," Linvall said, in genuine shock and horror. "If Marcia found out that I'd been lying on your behalf, there would be hell to pay. Anyway, why should I be doing you any favours?"

"Because you need me. You see, Marcia's told me about your minuscule willy, and I'm the only one here who can solve your problem."

Linvall was incensed. Where did Marcia get off . . .? He was intrigued, too.

"If my piece was small, I'm not saying it is," he began tentatively, "but if it were, what makes you so sure that you can help?"

"Because I used to have a minuscule willy, too. Tiny it was. Now, though, well, it's not so much that I'm well-endowed, it's just that I've got a huge penis . . ."

The wedding reception was to be at a grand mansion in 20 acres of its own well-maintained and impressive grounds in Harrow. There would be at least a thousand people there, more guests than at the church service. Gussie had hired a large marquee to be set on the lawn.

But Gussie hadn't only invited the cream of the crop. Every section of the community was represented amongst his friends and family. From the ordinary ragamuffin to the high society crew. From beauticians to musicians, some who only went to church at easter Some were single and free, glamourous and glitterous. Others were couples with the obligatory two-point-four. Everybody was well dressed, modelling the latest styles and designs. They all looked happy, with smiles on their faces, cracking jokes and laughing as they chatted with friends they hadn't seen for years.

" . . .Oh, didn't you know, he fell off a building . . .

tragic accident . . . he was a beautiful young brother . ." went one conversation.

"You really are a remarkably pretty piece of flesh, be sure to let me know whenever you get that urge," went another.

"Thanks for the time and the watch and the link, but you and I are history." Yet another.

"Yes, baby, you can feel, but the question is, can you taste?"

And another.

" 'Cause when my man asks for my hand, yeah, he'll want me for me and my savoir-faire/je ne sais quoi, yeah, and not an altered me who he won't be able to see in a few years. He'll also buy me expensive gear . . ."

Many of the movers and shakers were there also. A multi-million dollar 'think-tank' of black dignitaries selected from the very best pedigree, included a couple of MPs, a tribal chief in traditional African costume, and a peer of the realm — Lord Randall — who staggered around the worst for wear reeking of spilled whisky. You wouldn't think that Gussie had paid him a hefty attendance fee to secure his presence.

Also present were TV chef and child actor Elroy Bailey, soccer star Frank Marshall, television news presenter Marva Grant, a line of male models, hired strictly as 'props' for the day, and three press photographers lucky enough to be in on the scoop.

Amongst the other guests were ex-lovers, ex-friends, ex-husbands. Behind their nice smiles they looked about them suspiciously, collecting rumour, gossip and innuendo and observing the rivals who had now taken their places. There was an ex-wife, a secret admirer, trapped in a nightmare, opening up old wounds as her eyes met her ex's and, once again, every inch of her being ached to be with him. *This wasn't supposed to be happening!* She had vowed never ever to have anything to do with a black man again.

"I hate being single, I hate being single," she muttered to herself. "I hate being single, I hate being single, I hate being single . . ." she continued as if she was rehearsing the lines for a Hollywood movie.

As they arrived the old folks went straight into the church to rest their weary feet. Most of the younger generation preferred to hang around outside. It was a nice sunny day and, besides, they wanted to check out who was who was who was who, as each and every person arrived.

Not everybody present was there for the wedding. Several of the young businesssmen and women in attendance never missed an opportunity to network, be it a wedding, a funeral or a christening.

"It's all hush-hush at the moment," one of them was saying. "This is a billion dollar deal. But you've got to keep it quiet, I don't want anything messing up my chances . . ."

Linvall was wondering where Lacquan had got to when he spotted his spar.

"Yaow, Beres!" Linvall called out.

Beres spun to see him.

"Linvall, how are you doing?"

"Yeah-yeah," Linvall answered. "What's up with you?"

"Yeah, you know. By the way, I just saw your woman round the back of the church, walking arm in arm with some man. Big guy. They didn't look like they were just good friends, either."

Beres had hardly finished speaking before Linvall saw Marcia making her way towards him, Amos beside her.

"Speak of the devil." Wrong choice of words, Beres. "I was just telling Linvall that you were here."

Marcia turned to Beres, gave him that gorgon look that said, 'Scram, before I turn you into stone.'

Nuff said. Beres was gone.

"I just bumped into, Lacquan," Marcia said. "He said you've got something to tell me."

"Something to tell you?" Linvall stuttered. "No, no, not at all."

"So, you're accusing the boy of lying," Amos said, with a big cheesy grin.

"No, but he's mistaken."

"Are you sure?" Amos said. "Are you sure *you're* not lying. Your eyes look a bit shifty to me.

"Look, just get lost. This has nothing to do with you," Linvall retorted.

"Temper, temper," the detective said, giving him a wink in lieu of an oscar. "You've got a nice woman there," he said, contradicting Linvall's immediate thoughts. "That's what I can't understand about all you baby fathers. You have the nicest women in the world to take care of you and your pickney, yet you don't seem to appreciate it . . ."

"Well if you haven't got anything to say to me," Marcia said, "I certainly have something to say to you. "I believe Amos spent the night at your place."

"Yes . . . that's right."

"So that's your long, blonde hair on his suit?"

"Blonde? No . . ."

"While I've got you here, could you also explain how it is that my husband left home yesterday morning with his underpants the right way around, but when he got home they were back to front . . .?"

Linvall spluttered for several moments but couldn't come up with a feasible explanation.

Amos was grateful for Linvall's support minutes earlier, and when he found himself using the adjacent cubicle to his saviour in the men's toilet at the back of the church, he started treating Linvall like an old friend — his best friend — and confidante. He promised that he would show Linvall how to get the biggest, hugest, thickest stonker in the world.

"That's what I like about you," Amos kept telling him, "you're a man's man — the sort of guy you can be frank with. Like your wife, for example, she's okay and everything, she's a beautiful woman, charming, and she's excellent in bed. She's everything a man dreams about, but how can I tell her that I can't resist a woman with breasts? I just can't resist. You know what I mean? I guess, at the end of the day, all men really are dogs. Woof-woof!"

Inside, the north-west London church was filling up rapidly. The groom's family, conservatively dressed in suits and formal dresses, sat on one side of the aisle. Gussie's sister Evelyn and her husband Beckford cut a picture of the perfect buppie legal couple. Having removed his white panama hat as decorum would have it, Mr. Pottinger, Gussie's father, still looked positively colonial in his spotless white khaki suit. Both he and Mrs. P. looked relieved to see that their son seemed finally to be settling down for good.

Up in the gallery a gospel choir hummed a verse of praise to the most high. It was so beautiful, planned to every last detail, that there were already tears in the aisle.

Carmel's invitation list was much smaller. As most of her family had refused to attend, she only had her sister Amy, Amy's husband, and a handful of cousins in attendance, all blond-haired and blue-eyed, each wondering why anyone in their family should choose for a husband, someone who seemed as far from their race as an eskimo is from an Englishman. The rest of her guests were friends, nearly all of whom were meeting Gussie for the first time.

* * *

While the guests were arriving at the church, Carmel and her mother Millicent were still back at her flat on the other side of town, trying to convince each other to see the other's point of view. In a break with tradition,

Carmel had wanted her mother to give her away. Had begged her to do so, but Millicent simply reminded her daughter of how many times she had begged her not to marry this gaseous man.

" . . .And furthermore Gassie's got no class," Millicent was saying. This was her last ditch attempts at the eleventh hour to make her daughter see reason. She didn't know how, but somehow, despite all the evidence to the contrary, Gassie had managed to convince her daughter that he was worth marrying.

"It's becoming increasingly difficult for me to envision him in your ideal life. Deep inside, Carmel, you must know that he will never be the kind of husband you desire. Perhaps he knows this, too."

Carmel heard, but wasn't going to take her mother's bait, couldn't bring herself to talk about it anymore, wanted to ignore her. She had other things on her mind. Her views about life were changing. Although she didn't believe everything Gussie told her anymore, she did believe he wanted to spend the rest of his life with her. That was good enough for her.

Carmel had decided not to allow life to beat her down as it had done her mother.Where was the woman Millicent De Souza could have been? If only she could sever the shackles which held her captive to her past, dreaming that, "One day, I'll strike it rich again, one day my ship will come in."

* * *

Johnny was in the prime of his life. He had mapped out his future years ago and was now firmly en route down the grand highway to success. He was a winner and had the potential to become one of the most successful black businessmen out there. As far as he was concerned, nothing was going to stand between him and that pot of gold at the end of the rainbow. He planned to retire at 35 and buy an island in the Caribbean on which he would invite all these buppy girls to come and spend time with him.

Like Hyacinth, the mystery woman he had been chasing in his car for weeks. She had called him up. Said that she got his number from the hotel porter. That she heard he was looking for her.

"But aren't you looking for me?" Johnny asked. After all, it was she who had made all the moves so far.

"Well, yes," came a sultry, seductive voice down the line, "I'm looking for a man like you. Do you think you can fill all my requirements."

"Try me," Johnny had replied confidently. "You'll find that I can fill anything . . ."

To high society women like Hyacinth, Johnny knew, he was just a bit of rough. But a bit of rough with intelligence, someone they could relate to. There wasn't much hope of that nowadays with the abysmal state of guys out there. He was charming and witty and kept them smiling all evening. He knew what a woman needed by way of convivial atmosphere, and he provided it. He could talk about almost anything under the sun, even things he knew very little about.

Sometimes, women are prepared to pay dearly for a man who can do that.

He had invited her to Gussie's wedding for their first date.

They had taken his car and, of course, he had made every effort to get up close and personal on the journey. But Hyacinth wasn't playing ball. She was indignant. Told him to keep his hands to himself and elbowed him away. So persistent was Johnny in his advances and so determined was she that he wouldn't be getting any tonight, that she found it necessary to discuss the heaviness of her menstrual flow with him. That soon cooled his desire.

They got to the church late. By now all the guests were inside, waiting the imminent arrival of the bride. As they approached the wrought iron gate to the church, Johnny tried to snake his arm once more around Hyacinth's coca-cola bottle waist. This time, she didn't play. She spun round like a whirlwind and delivered a perfect roundhouse kick to his head with the skill, strength and suppleness of someone who practices the ancient art of kung fu every day. Before Johnny knew what hit him, she had pulled a pair of handcuffs out of thin air, seemingly, and snapped them around his wrist and the gate.

"Hey, what's the big idea?" Johnny cried out.

Hyacinth merely stood back, pulled out a mobile phone and made a call.

"Let me out of here," Johnny cried. "This ain't funny. The joke is over."

Hyacinth said nothing. She simply waited and watched.

Outside the church, an open top horse drawn carriage pulled up outside the church. It took Johnny a few seconds to register the face. He couldn't believe it. Gussie was marrying Carmel, a woman he himself had been having a little on-off thing with last year. He remembered it fondly, he could still taste her on the tip of his tongue.

"Somebody better call God, 'cause he's missing an angel," someone called out from the back of the church. Suddenly, without warning, the organist started playing *The Wedding March*, accompanying the bride's arrival.

As irresistible as all the other ladies in the church were, Carmel was clearly the queen of the ball. She was a knockout. Looked a million dollars in a designer wedding dress that Gussie had had made for her at no small expense. There was a clearly audible gasp as she stepped into the church, with her uncle at her side.

As he stood nervously at the altar in the packed church, waiting for his bride to come alongside him, tender thoughts of love-warmed hearts and a mellow mood, were some of the images that filled Gussie's mind. He used to be a heartbreaker, lovemaker, back breaker even, but now he was sitting on a mountain of love. All he ever dreamed of was a woman who could give him love until it overflowed.

Tonight, in their honeymoon compartment on the Trans-Siberian Express, their love would overflow. They would dance naked in the moonlight, the aroma of their bodies intertwined. As he woke from his daydreaming, a slender, manicured finger reached out and touched him. For a moment they stood, gazing into each other's eyes, synchronised breathing on stand-by.

"Baby, you look better and better each day," he whispered. "Right now, you look like tomorrow."

As they knelt before the altar, a photographer came up with his camera. As he took a couple of pics, he gave Carmel a knowing wink and licked his lips seductively.

Gussie had seen it. "Who's that?" he whispered.

"Oh, it's just an ex-boyfriend of mine," Carmel whispered back.

Free-I, the rastaman, was as surprised as everyone else that he had been invited to the wedding. He hadn't expected it. He had been personally asked by the groom to add a touch of old fashion exotica to the blessing alongside the officiating pastor. Though that created a lot of controversy behind the scenes, Gussie's wishes were fulfilled.

From the altar, with bride and groom kneeling before him, Free-I said his piece.

"This marriage is not just the coming together of two, as one, under the sight of God," he declared declared to the attentive congregation. "These two people before me represent the coming together of a people who have been taken and scattered far and wide." Then turning to Carmel and Gussie, Free-I continued.

"Behold, your love as a door to another world. But true love don't come easy. The nectar flows from time to time. Woman, I beg you stick to your man. Don't worship diamonds, don't worship pearls. Gussie, you fe 'member, man smart but the woman smarter. Give her your loving, don't forget about the hugging and teasing. Don't forget about the all night squeezing. Do not mistreat your wife. Such family rows are a disgrace to the Emperor. Do not seduce the wives of other men. Be humble. Let your ears hear advice. If you alone drink a medicine for long life, or to stave off death, you will be left alone in the wasteland."

Then he turned back to Carmel. "As for you, do not be lazy. Behind every successful man there is a supportive and understanding woman. You have to support Gussie and understand that he doesn't always have time to devote to the relationship. The only way to success is through hard, hard work and plenty of faith. Give thanks and praises to the most high. Your relationship from here on will evolve into one between two adults assuming their own individual responsibilities. I will be there to lend you both as much emotional support as I can, but that is as far as I can extend myself," he explained. Please be careful, and if you can't, be true."

Outside the church, Johnny was still trying to sweet talk Hyacinth into uncuffing him. She listened but didn't say a word. Waiting.

Finally somebody emerged from inside the church.

"Well, well . . . Mr. Dollar. We meet again."

"You again!" Johnny's voice was exasperated. "I thought I told you to piss off."

"You can't get rid of me that easily. I see you're

already acquainted to my associate Hyacinth Criss, one of the best undercover private investigators in the business. Good work, Criss."

Private investigator!

"Look, I've had enough of you," Johnny said.

"You've had enough of me? I've had enough of you, so calm down and behave yourself. I've had to chase all over town for you, so don't make me get ignorant."

"You want a piece of me?"

"I didn't say that?"

"You want a piece of me?" Johnny repeated.

Amos laughed. "Don't make me laugh," he said. "You wouldn't get very far against me with both hands, let alone one tied behind your back. Just keep quiet."

With that he turned his back on Johnny and went back into the church, leaving Hyacinth to keep guard.

Back inside the church, Beres was feeling as guilty as hell, in fact he felt ashamed. He couldn't believe who Gussie's bride was. Why, he got off with her only last night, on her hen night, when she was as drunk as a skunk. He had still been trying to find that elusive orgasm, willing to try anything or anyone that could help. He had met her at a bar, where she was getting sloshed with a brace of her women friends. She had given him the eye, and he had returned the compliment. Somehow, they managed to give her friends the slip and sneak off to her loft apartment in Shoreditch.

What did he really know about her? Nothing much. Nothing at all. To his delight, he was able to come for the first time in months. What a pleasant surprise, this woman had whatever it was that his ex-wife had which could make him enjoy an orgasm.

In the background, Beres heard the echo of the pastor's voice as he asked if there was anyone present who knew of any reason why this union should not take place. The little voice in Beres' left ear was telling him to remain seated. To keep his mouth shut. To think of what it could do to his friend if he spoke up now. The little voice in his right ear was urging him to wave the sword of truth and speak up in the name of justice and British fair play. He couldn't allow his best friend to marry a woman that he himself was sleeping with less than twenty-four hours previously. Moreover, she was one of those rare woman who could make him come and, understandably, Beres wanted her for himself . . .

Outside the church, Johnny's problems were not over. Cutty had been driving by when he saw him handcuffed to the gate. He stopped his car and climbed out.

"You raas, you," he called out as he approached Johnny. "I've been looking for you everywhere. My missus is pregnant, you know. And you're the raas what done it. Forget about that small change, business. It's going to cost fifty grand for me to even consider not rearranging your face with my ratchet."

END . . .for now.